MCCULLOUGH'S JAMBOREE BOOK 6

KATHI S. BARTON

This is a work of fiction. Names, characters, places, and incidents are products of the author's imagination or are used fictitiously and are not to be construed as real. Any resemblance to actual events, locations, organizations, or persons, living or dead, is entirely coincidental.

World Castle Publishing, LLC
Pensacola, Florida
Copyright © Kathi S. Barton 2018
Paperback ISBN: 9781629899589
eBook ISBN: 9781629899596
First Edition World Castle Publishing, LLC, July 23, 2018
http://www.worldcastlepublishing.com

Licensing Notes

Cover: Karen Fuller
Editor: Maxine Bringenberg

CHAPTER 1

Jamie figured she'd give it ten more minutes, then she was leaving. She'd been at the hospital longer than she thought was necessary for fainting. Well, she'd really just passed out from shock, but she'd never done that before. Tossing off the cover that had been on her when she woke, she heard the baby crying so close that she ventured out of the room she'd been in and followed the sound. Her heart broke for how pitiful the tiny person's voice sounded.

There were ten babies in varying ages in the bassinets, all of them under six months old, she'd bet, and asleep but for the child that had her finding them. Lifting the little girl from the bassinet, she sat in the nearby chair and started rocking her.

"I have been looking for you for so long, I thought that I'd been mistaken about it." Rocking a little more, the baby quieted down and stared up at her with the most beautiful green eyes that she'd ever seen. "There is this guy here—you'll know him as soon as you see him—who is a bully. And he's a big hulking sort of person. Not like he's stupid or anything—

at least he didn't sound that way. But he's big, like that green guy that used to be on television. I know you wouldn't know who that is, but I'm just making a reference."

The baby's tiny hand wrapped around her finger and she smiled. Jamie loved babies — all kids really, but babies had a special place in her heart reserved just for them. When the baby's eyes started to close a little at a time, Jamie decided to talk to her more.

"When I was a little girl, I was dropped off at one of those safe places. I'm not sure why anyone would think that it was safe. I spent the next five years there, and let me tell you, it was not a place I'd go back to even on a threat of death. Then I ended up where no one should ever be allowed to stay. It was horrific, and the things they did to me were twice that bad." Jamie heard the door near where she was sitting open and then close. "Anyway, the place. It wasn't a baby mill like you were in, at least I don't think so. But a real place that unwanted children went. I say unwanted because we were told that every day — that we were there because no one wanted us for one reason or another. But the lab did. They needed me for a lot of things that I didn't want to do. So that's where I grew up. I think the place has shut down now. The house was a showstopper, really beautiful if a little out of date, and I loved it. Just not the people there."

She looked up when the curtain was thrown back. There stood her nemesis with a gun pointed at her again. Jamie started to stand and give him a big part of her mind when he slipped the gun back in wherever he'd gotten it from and sat down on the floor in front of her.

"I thought I'd just sit here in the event you wanted to hit me again. This way I'm closer to the floor already." She wanted to stick her tongue out at him, but knew that he'd laugh at her. "You said that your name is James. Why would anyone mistake you for a male? I'm Hawk, or Hawkins if you prefer."

"I was a great deal younger back then, you idiot. Don't you have someone else you can harass? I mean, I was having a nice conversation with this little girl, and you—"

"Her name is Lily, Lily Anderson. Her parents are on their way to see her. All the children have names now." She just looked down at Lily, and her heart hurt to know that someone loved her. "Why do you think that no one loves you?"

"You're reading my mind. Why the hell would you think that isn't rude?" He just shrugged and leaned back on his elbow, smiling at her. "What are you in here for, besides pulling yet another gun on me?"

"I only pulled one out on you. The first time, it wasn't meant for you but the guy holding you." She rolled her eyes at him and started rocking again, anything to get the man to leave her alone. "You aren't afraid of me; that's a first. Usually people who've just met me never hit me in the face. Then you hit me in my balls too."

"Perhaps it's because you're nicer to others than you have been me." Kicking his foot away from the front of the rocker, she glared at him. "I swear to Christ, you have to go away. I don't like you one bit, and you're taking up all my air while you're here."

"You're not human." Jamie felt every part of her body tense up. Then she looked for a way to escape. "I'm not sure what you are, but you're not going anywhere now."

"Why is that? And let me remind you that I've hurt you twice now. If I want to leave, then I will. You won't be able to

7

stop me." He looked at the exit door and she did as well. There were men standing in front of it, and she could tell they were armed. "You're holding me prisoner? What the fuck for?"

"They're here for the children. And for me." She asked him if he was going to be arrested. "You're very defensive; anyone ever tell you that before? No, they're not here to arrest me. They work for me. I'm considered a big deal by some people."

"Whatever." She stood up, and he was suddenly standing too. Like he'd just willed it or something. "You're a cat. Jaguar, I'm guessing. I could have told you that before you were shooting at me, but I was distracted. By you telling Ben to shoot me."

"That was before I knew you." She pointed out that he didn't know her now. "True. But I'm hoping that we can remedy that soon."

She was missing something in what he was saying, but she was too stressed to figure it out. Putting Lily back in her crib, she moved to leave the same way that she'd come in, by the back door. When she opened it up, there were three men standing there with the woman from the house. Miss Laughs a Lot.

The two in uniform aimed their guns at her and she backed up a couple of steps. And right into the arms of Hawk. She struggled to get away from him, thinking that she'd be safer with the guns pointed at her, when Miss Laughs a Lot told them to stand down. No one moved.

"Did you hear me, soldiers? I said to stand down." Neither man moved, but they were looking at the man behind her. "Hawk, you're going to lose these two idiots if you don't make them behave around me. My word is my bond."

"Stand down." Both put their guns to their sides when Hawk said for them to do it with a great deal of authority in his voice. The other man laughed. Miss Laughs a Lot didn't seem to find it funny. Getting out of Hawk's embrace was a good deal easier now. "They work for me and only me. This was a good test for them. Thanks, Burcher."

"It wasn't a trial for anything, you fucking bastard. I don't care for being ignored. Perhaps they don't know me." She turned to both men and they were nodding like their heads had somehow come loose from their necks. "So, you do know me. That doesn't explain to me why when I give you an order, you don't obey."

"They're not dogs. Christ, you got your panties in a twist because they didn't listen to the great Burcher, or whatever the fuck your name is? You on some power trip, or are you always a fucking cunt?" Every one of the men backed up from her and Burcher. "You might get a lot more done if you ask politely when you want something to go your way. Like, and this is just an example, 'Would you mind putting your guns down? I don't want any more bloodshed—'"

Jamie was lifted from the floor by Burcher. She was holding her there like she didn't weigh a thing. Hawkins reached out to touch Lauren when the third man got right up and in his face. Jamie did the only thing she could think of before she passed out from lack of air. She shifted.

Her beast roared when she told her to calm the fuck down. The people were afraid of her, that she could see, but she really didn't care. Right now, she needed to get out of there before they spoke to someone about her.

The presence of another being felt calming. Even the beast inside of her seemed to know that someone less than but like her was coming. Before the door opened, she as her beast, a great black bear—bigger than any normal—moved away from it. Whatever was coming, it wasn't angry, but it was concerned.

As soon as he walked through the door, she knew him for what he was. Not a name, but she and him had been created at the lab. When he came toward her, talking softly the whole time, Jamie whimpered. He wasn't close to as powerful as she was, but she knew he had a great deal more than she did in knowledge of what he could do. She'd love to learn from him, but that would be dangerous. She could hurt him.

"Hello. I thought that all the others were found. I had no idea that you were there." She let the bear go and stood before him. He was taller than her by a few inches, but nothing near what Hawkins was. "May I take your hand in mine?"

"No. Don't touch me." He nodded and put his hands behind his back. "I saw you there. In the room when I'd look around at night."

"Jon?" He glanced at Hawk when he said his name. Then Jon looked at the others with a smile. The servicemen were guarding the door again and didn't appear as if they gave a shit about what was going on around them. "Is she like you? Someone from the lab?"

"No. She's very different than I am. Just as dangerous, but no less hurt by the men there." She watched Hawk when he moved to come closer to her. "I wouldn't, Hawk. Not yet at any rate."

"She's my mate, Jon." No one said a word but seemed to focus all their eyes on her. She lifted her chin and decided it was well past time for her to get the fuck out of there. "What do you mean, she's very different than—?"

"And *she's* standing right the fuck here. You are the rudest man I've ever had the misfortune to meet. I'm leaving here." Jon asked her to wait. "For what? For them to call someone and tell them where I am? Thanks, but no thanks. I've been down that road more times than I'd like to think about.

"Tell them what you are." She looked at Jon then at Hawk. Jamie knew what a mate was, but there was no way that anyone would want her after what she'd been through. "You'd be very surprised at what these people can do for you."

"I was dropped off at the home for wayward kids when I was an infant. During my first five years, I was a troubled child." Hawk snorted. "Fuck you. What would you have done if you became a monster that didn't have any idea where she was? I was a bear shifter and didn't have any idea how to control her." She looked at the floor, anywhere but at Hawk. "I wasn't one of the lab rats like you were. I wasn't a human when I was taken there at the age of five—I was a shifter, so I guess that qualified for me to be discarded when they were done with me. Taken from the home I had been in since birth. After a while they got tired of me not doing what they wanted, and I was put away to be destroyed. When I slipped out of the cage they had me in, I wandered around the building to keep up with what they were doing."

"They messed with you with drugs too, then." She nodded at the man near Lauren. "I'm Colin McCullough. Lauren is my wife. And Hawkins is my brother. He's Army."

"Yeah, I got that part." Jamie ignored Hawk. She looked at Jon and spoke only to him. "They did the first experiments on me, before you were given anything. The trouble was, no one took into consideration that I hadn't been human, so they

11

would affect me differently than you. Second, I was a way for them to figure out if whatever they were set to give you would maybe kill you. And if it didn't me, then they'd give it to you."

"You were five when they did this to you?" She told Jon how they'd find her every month or so then use her again. "They knew where you were at all times, I'm thinking. The men there only gave you the illusion that you were free to roam."

Hawkins watched her. He knew as surely as he was standing there she was going to bolt. And he'd bet any kind of money that he'd not be able to find her unless she allowed it. Marking her wouldn't do him much good either. She was just as strong, if not stronger than Jon, Hawkins would bet.

"I have to go. No, I'm going to go now. I only stuck around here to find the babies." Lauren stepped in front of her. "Do you have a death wish? I would have thought someone with your obvious training would know not to stand in front of a dangerous bullet."

"Is that what you are? Dangerous? I'm not so afraid of you. More that I'm afraid of what they did to you." Jamie put up her hand and morphed it into a gun. Then a sword. And again she turned her hand into a monster, long claws and all. "Nope, not going to work. You're his mate, and that means something to this family."

"Well, it means shit to me." Jamie looked at him before speaking again. "I'm nothing you want to fuck with or fuck. I am dangerous, and I'm not as stupid as some people may think I am. I will hurt you if you try again to detain me."

"I'm asking you to please not leave me." She shook her

head and glanced at the doors again. He knew her plan to leave was rapidly coming to fruition. "I'm asking you to take a chance here. No one will be able to touch you again. I will swear this on my life."

"And you? Will you claim me? I'm guessing that's what you think is going to happen. And you might be immortal, but removing your head will be easy enough for me." He nodded and told her that he knew that she was stronger than him. "Hell, I'm stronger than even Jon is. Don't you get it? I'm nothing more than a taste tester from long ago. If I lived, then they would inject the shit into him. Sometimes more than once."

"I don't care about any of that. I was bemoaning the fact that someday my mate would come to me. Basically because of what I do. I'm not such a cup of tea either." He moved closer all the time, hoping that if he could touch her once, his cat would feel much better. "You know what I am. A jaguar first and foremost. My cat is pissy with me, because he too knows who you are to us."

"Again, I don't care." She looked at the exit then back at him just before he was able to touch her. Hawk felt himself being tossed back. Hitting the wall behind him, he braced himself for whatever came next. He was sure, too, that there would be more put upon him.

Hawkins watched her while she calmed herself. She'd not lost total control, he knew that, but had punched him with just enough magic to keep him away from her. Sitting up, he stayed there while the rest of them left. Even his men walked out the door.

"You did that? Made them leave us?" She nodded. "And can you make me leave too? Or is it the mate thing that prevents you from making me do anything I don't want to? By the way, you're not supposed to be able to hurt me. I guess we can chalk that up to being a falsehood."

"I can't make you leave. Had I been able to, then you'd be gone. And no, it doesn't have anything to do with you thinking I'm your mate." She looked down at her arm where he'd touched her, and he could see the marks on her arm.

Standing up and going to her, he asked her if she was all right. Then he pulled her arm over to have a better look at what had happened. She was burned. Like his fingers brushing over her, and that had been all it was, had caused her to blister and be in pain.

"Why did you touch me? I told you, several times, not to touch." He let her arm go but didn't back away this time. "I don't want to be here."

"No, I got that." He laughed a little, and saw a tease of a smile on her mouth. Then she became hard again. "Why did you burn when I touched you? And why not the second time that I held up your arm?"

"You were intending to detain me. For lack of a better word, my programming knew that and lashed out at you. The second time you weren't as aggressive. I didn't need to harm you again." Hawkins nodded and touched his fingers to her cheek. "That doesn't mean that I won't fucking hurt you. Go away. And then I will. You'll be much happier without me around, trust me. I know this for a fact."

"There have been others that you hurt?" Instead of answering him, she walked to the window and looked out. "I can help you. You can tell, I'm assuming, that I'm a bit more than a cat. I'm in no way as powerful as the two of you, you and Jon, but I can hold my own."

14

"They won't care what you are, if you have loved ones, or are even an immortal. They'll take you apart right there along with me once they figure it out." He shivered, thinking of all the shit she'd had done to her. "I'm trying my best to save you, and you're too dense to understand that forgetting about me will be the best thing that happens to you."

"Doubtful. I mean, I was afraid of when I found my mate. Not afraid but concerned that I'd been too long in the military and might not be good for a woman. Hell, I'm barely good to my family on a daily basis. I can see you have no trouble putting me in my place and making sure that I understand when you're pissed off." She didn't laugh like he had hoped she would. "I'm not a gentle man. I don't know how to be romantic. I haven't the first clue how dating works anymore. When I was seventeen I signed on to become something more. What I hadn't counted on was Burcher finding me and recruiting me for her team."

"I'm assuming that was her last name before becoming McCullough. I'd toss her into a deep hole or cage and lock the door, but that's just me." He told her what her name was before. "Colonel Lauren Burcher? I knew that she was something more than just a woman. She's a bitch."

"Yeah, she might say the same about you. But she'd be happy with it instead of pissed off like you are." She looked like she didn't understand, and he'd bet she didn't want to. "I was called Mac in the service. My family is the only people that call me Hawkins. Or sometimes Hawk when I'm not in too much trouble with them."

She didn't say the obvious next line of "that must happen a lot then." Hawkins realized that she was going to forever do the unexpected and not care a bit if it offended or even pissed someone off. She was a great deal like Lauren, but Jamie would be meaner when pressed, he guessed.

"Why don't you come home with me?" She turned and looked at him then. "I have a nice house. My brother helped me buy it when I was in the service."

"You still are. In the service, I mean." He nodded, not saying anything. "I'm not going home with you. I have one that I like well enough. But you're to stay away from me. I don't want to get involved with you at all."

"I'm afraid it's too late for that." He pulled her body to him and was surprised that he didn't hurt her again. Pressing his mouth to hers, hoping that she'd allow him a taste of her, he moaned when she finally did.

Her body fit his. When he held her closer, letting her feel what she was doing to him, he thought he would happily die right now the way she'd wrapped her arms around him. Before he could lift her up from the floor, find a hard place to lay her while he feasted on her body, she pulled her mouth away from his.

"I'm sorry."

He started to tell her that she had nothing to be sorry about when she disappeared. Hawk was left holding air, and was no closer to finding anything out than he had been before. And Hawk wanted to know everything. Reaching to Burcher, he asked her if she'd do him a favor.

If you're going to ask me if I can find out something about your girl, I'm already on it. Your mate is a piece of work, by the way. She isn't the least bit impressed with me, nor does she care that I could snap her like a twig. Hawk wisely said nothing. He was reasonably sure that Jamie could not just snap Lauren, but get rid of the body without any trouble. *There isn't much when I do a regular search, but I'm digging. Where is she, by the way?*

Gone. She was here, then vanished. I need to talk to Jon too. Maybe he can shed some light on things. Lauren said she doubted it. *Yeah, that's what I'm thinking too. I might have to return to Washington, but I'll be in contact with you while I'm gone. I'm assuming that Mom and Dad know that I've found my mate?*

Yes, but it wasn't me. I was really pissed about that too. Colin told them before I was able to. She paused for too long, but he knew better than to hurry her along. *Hawk, your mate is really in the shit. She's not just wanted by some very unsavory people, but there is a warrant out for her arrest as well. Murder and robbery. But they know her as an entirely different name. Holly Tree. Even I can tell that's a fake, and I'm not looking very hard.*

I'll need what you can find. I don't have a clue where she is, or even if she needs a place to stay. But she's my mate, and for what it's worth, I'm sorry I ever doubted that I wanted one. She said that she'd have it couriered to him. *Thanks. I owe you one.*

Never, Mac. Never that. I owe you so much, I don't think being immortal is ever going to be long enough to pay you back for most of it. He said nothing. *I'm printing it up now and making arrangements to have it brought to you. Should be there by this evening.*

Hawk could disappear too. He didn't care for doing it, because when he reappeared, he had to be careful where he was landing, so to speak. But this time he had no choice. He should have been in Washington yesterday. He only had a few more missions to go before he was done with everything military. For the first time in his life, he wasn't dreading it.

CHAPTER 2

Jamie was going to find the men looking for her and take care of them. She was frankly sick to death of all this cat and mouse shit. Not that she had any idea why these particular men wanted her; she just knew that it had to end now.

Reaching out beyond where she was, she found two of the four men not too far away. This was good, she thought, and willed her body there.

"Holy fuck." She just cocked a brow at the man who spoke. "They didn't tell us that you could fade in the woodwork like that, then come out and scare us. We've been hunting for you for a while now."

"Yes, I'm aware of your clumsy attempts at trying to find me. Why, is what I want to know. Why do you even care where I am?" The second man started for his gun, and Jamie lifted him up so that he was on the ceiling. "Answer me."

"We were only told to not hurt you in any way. Nor was we to touch you without your consent. I'm guessing you're not too keen on that either." She shook her head and told the first man to sit down. "Yes ma'am, I can do that. Are you by chance going to come quietly with us? We sure could use the money that is attached to bringing you in."

"No, I'm not going anywhere quietly with you or your moron friend." He looked up at the guy on the ceiling. "Would you like to join him? If not, tell me who is sending out what I'm assuming is the cream of the crop to find me."

He looked at her, confused. She didn't have time to tell him what she'd meant, and asked him again who had sent them. This shit was going to stop now.

"His name? I don't know. He had this application online that said how they were looking for a woman and they'd pay well to whoever found her." He grinned. "I could take your picture with me and then he'd have to give me something, don't you think?"

"No, you're not taking my picture. You want to know why? Because you'd be just stupid enough to think that he's ever going to pay you whether you bring me in or not." He told her that he'd promised. "Yes, I'm sure. Because people who put ads on the computer and pay way too much to find me are going to be the most honest people around. He's going to kill you. Whoever he is, you're as good as dead. Once he figures out that I'm caught, the rest of you will die so he doesn't have any witnesses."

"Nah, you can't be right about that. He said he'd pay us." Jamie gave up and looked around the room. "You wanting to have a seat? We just ordered us some dinner, and it'll be up soon enough."

"Did he give you a phone? Do you still have the email that he sent you, if that's how he contacts you?" Idiot said that he did and got up to hand her the phone. Then he went to the laptop and brought up the email. "You can read it right there if you want. See how he's saying over and over that he'll pay whoever brings you in."

Touching her fingers to the email, she was tracking where it came from when she felt someone else doing the same. Reaching out to whoever it was, she cursed for a good minute before finishing the search of the address of the computer the man had used. When she had it, she reached out to Lauren and asked her what the fuck she was doing.

I'm sure that you're aware that someone is trying to find you. So, I'm looking for the IP address so I can look like the hero to you, and maybe you'll be more respectful to me. I am a badass, you know. Jamie told her the address she was hunting for as well as the phone number. *How the fuck did you get that before me? I'm telling you, Jamie, I'm liking you more and more with each passing moment.*

Leave this alone. You're only going to bring some next level shit down on your head, and that will bring in more people. You don't know what you're fucking with here. Lauren told her to tell her. *You really want to know everything about me? I'm telling you right now, it's not pretty or very nice.*

Yes, I do want to know. That way I can tell whether or not we can become BFFs or not. Lauren was going to be the death of her, she knew it. *Who is this person that you're hunting for, and what does he have to do with two men in the hotel in Indiana?*

I'm here with the idiots now. And if the person looking for me is anything like these guys, I can hide right out in the open and they'll never find me. She had a feeling they were a distraction, for her to follow up on so that she could be found. *They're trying to find me for reasons that you can't understand.*

I'm pretty smart, so lay it on me.

Jamie left the two men in the hotel, bound and gagged,

21

to go to where Lauren was. Calling in the police to come and take them away was the only way to keep them from being murdered. There was enough hardware and weapons in the room that they'd be in jail for a while.

She was alone in the big office, and Jamie wanted to keep it that way. Taking away her ability to reach out to anyone, she felt safer than she had in recent weeks.

"That's a neat trick you have there. You said you were in Indiana, yet here you are a few seconds later. Are you going to talk to me, or do I have to rough you up a bit first?"

Lauren laughed, and Jamie wondered if everyone knew just how insecure this woman was. Lauren was joking. But Jamie wasn't in the mood for it, nor for this woman trying to get into shit that was bigger than she was. Standing up, she started pacing the room when Lauren laughed. She asked her if she'd blocked her from talking to anyone else.

"Yes. Not that I don't trust you, but I do have trust issues with everyone. You were going to call in the troops, and one of them would have been Hawk. I'm not going there with him." Lauren nodded and leaned back in her chair. "Where to start.... All right. My real name is James Fitzpatrick. I change my name when it suits me, or someone knows it. I was named James by the proprietor of the children's home I was in. He hadn't checked on my gender and filled out my certificate wrong."

"Why use your real name this time?" Jamie told her that she used it from time to time. Just to throw them off. "Ah, I get it. If you are forever changing up your name, they'll think that one is a fake too. Good job. I would have thought of it sometime."

"Anyway. I was special in that I was really an orphan in

the place, but no one knew what had happened to my parents. The others were kids that they'd pick up off the streets. Not to do the humanitarian thing, but to have them for something else they had in mind. They'd give them a meal, and in exchange for the shitty stuff they'd been fed, they were chained to the bed, as I was, and sold for different projects that came along. I, however, wasn't ready to go anywhere until I was five. I put up a fuss when they tried. I used to be a bear. Now I'm everything."

"So are Jon and Mac. Though I don't think he's played around with his skills enough yet to know what he can be." Jamie knew that feeling. "So, you were taken to this lab where Jon was. For the sole purpose of using you as a test dummy?"

"No, not at first." She heard someone at the door and looked at Lauren. "You might as well let him in. This might keep him from pursuing anything with me."

The door opened, and Hawk was standing there. She wasn't starting over, and he seemed to know not to ask her to. When he was seated in the office's only other chair, Jamie picked up where she had left off.

"When I was first at the lab, I was getting injections every couple of hours. And on the days that they got a reaction from them, they'd celebrate like it was Christmas or some shit like that." Jamie looked at the wall in front of her, wondering what happened to all the underlings that had worked there.

"They're all dead." Jamie nodded, Lauren having answered her unspoken question. "There was some trouble for a little while afterwards, but we took care of it. That's what we do, work together to figure out how to make us all safe."

"And that's what I'm doing right now. Trying to make you see that you're unsafe while I'm here." Hawk stood up, then sat back down when Lauren told him to. "When I turned fifteen, things started to go haywire with their tests. I was also getting stronger than them, so they had to shoot me with a dart to knock me out before they'd feel safe enough to come into the cage to get me. That didn't last long either."

"You adapted to what they were giving you." She nodded at Hawk when he spoke softly. "You said that you were getting stronger. I'm assuming that you don't mean just your powers."

"No. I was physically stronger than anyone there, and I proved it on a daily basis. After a while I was let out of the cage. It was probably less expensive than replacing them every day. I did not like being confined." Hawk nodded. Jamie knew he would understand being confined and what it could do to a person like them. "When Jon escaped—I'm guessing that someone here helped him out—I was found and tied down with special chains. That too didn't last long, and before I left for the final time, I destroyed all the notes that I could find on me. As well as anything on the computer."

"So to us, who had the computers scanned and read, you didn't exist. That is a good trick too. Why?" Jamie asked Lauren what she meant. "Why do you care if your name is found out? It's not like you couldn't hide from them. Or better yet, kill them when they proved too close to you."

"What they did to me was my business. And when I left, I didn't want some fucked up government agency finding me and trying to make me into what they wanted." Hawk simply said a weapon. "Yes. I was supposed to be the next Jon. The one that got away. But the trouble with that was, I decided long before then that I wasn't going to be anything to anyone that I didn't want to be."

"What is it you can do that would be considered a weapon? I don't mean the fact that you can morph into anything, including larger weapons I'm assuming. But they must have known of one thing that kept you there for so long." She nodded and stared at Hawk. "Will you tell me?"

She nodded and stepped back from them. Closing her eyes because the light would hurt her a little, Jamie turned into the weapon that would end all strife for everyone. She would be used against every kind of enemy possible before they used her for their personal gain.

"Holy Christ." She let them come closer but didn't let them touch her. She could incinerate them with only a touch. "You can burn through armies and houses too. Is there more to you than this?"

She reached out with her heat and touched a paper on the desk. It burned and disappeared with the flame that she could control. But the desk and anything around it or on it was unharmed. Letting the flame go, she stood there and let them stare. Her heart hurt because she could see the excitement in their eyes. They'd sell her off in a moment if they thought that they could.

"I'm not excited because I know what I can do to you. I would never sell you to anyone or anything. But I am excited to know that you can take care of yourself and me if it came to that." She told Hawk that he should be terrified. "I would be if I knew that you were out there searching for me. I'm assuming that the people who are searching for you have no idea of what you can do, at least that part of it."

"No, they don't. Do you realize what I am? What I just turned into? I was a ball of the hottest fire ever known. I'm not just hot, I'm white hot. Things that I touch, including people, will be gone without a trace. And these fucking idiots think that they'll be able to corral me into doing what they want." Hawk nodded and sat down. He looked relaxed enough to take a nap. "You're being dense if you think this is a good thing. I can move into a home, burn only what I want, and get out without a single trace that I'd been there."

"I understand that more than you can know right now. I know what it's like to be thought of as only a weapon. Something that can be used to kill without being killed. I've been in plenty of situations that had me going into a person's home, killing the man or woman there, and getting out. And no one would know that he was dead until they checked on him. I'm that good." Jamie looked at Lauren when she nodded. "What you fail to understand about me—and that's all right, because we don't know each other that well—is that I just don't care what you can or can't do. You're my mate, and I will, if I'm able, protect you like I would hope that someday you would do for me."

Jamie wanted to stomp her foot and scream at him that he was being a fool. Just as she was thinking of something that she could do to him, to make him understand, she felt the danger.

"Get down." They both obeyed like she'd made them do it. Jamie reached out with her power and knew that the helicopter was coming for Lauren. Whatever she'd done, she'd pissed off the wrong people. Jamie looked at Lauren and realized that she might not know what she'd done either. "I'm going to have to destroy the men coming here. Don't move."

~*~

Hawk didn't know what to think about this. He was glad

that Jamie had been able to take the men out, but he was worried about her. She no more liked to kill than he did, it seemed. He looked over at her as she stood near him. They had come to the scene of the wreckage before the first police officer did.

"They were after Lauren. While they didn't know where she was, they had an idea that it might have been in the downtown area, not at her home." Hawk asked Jamie if she knew what they wanted. "Yes. She apparently stopped a shipment coming into port, and the men were pissed about it. One of them, a boss in the area, he was on the helicopter as well."

There was a helicopter there in the rubble of the accident. But the only way that he knew that was because he'd been told it was there. The wreckage was massive, yet it was contained. He wondered if Jamie was doing that now or if she'd done it when she'd pulled them out of the sky.

"His name was Jackson. I'm not sure what his first name was. That's all he was called by the man in the chopper with him." Hawk asked about the pilot. "He was no better than the boss that was there. He had a great deal of child porn on his computer that the police are going to find as soon as they identify them."

"How will they think this happened? I mean, they won't think that someone just pulled them out of the sky and pounded them into the earth, will they?" She looked at him, and he wondered if she knew just how beautiful she was. He decided now might not be the time to tell her that.

"They'll think it was a faulty engine. When they came down, instead of slowing, as it might have done if he could have controlled it, it accelerated and hit the ground harder than a normal fall would have done. No other people were hurt by this. I wouldn't do that." He said that he knew that. "Then why are you staring at me as if I have something in my teeth? If you see something, just fucking tell me."

"All right. I think you're stunning." She rolled her eyes at him. "You told me to tell you—I am. And while I love the way you dismiss any kind of compliment, I'm telling you what I was thinking when I was staring at you."

"Lauren was on a high when she said that to me. Glad that she was not hurt, or her family." Lauren had told Jamie that she was brilliant and that she was forever beholden to her. "And I'm not stunning. I'm just a person that has this incredible power."

"I think that you're as beautiful as anything I've ever seen. Once when I was overseas, I saw the sun coming up over the desert. The colors were blended together in such a way that it looked as if they faded one into the other. It was gorgeous. I have seen a lot of sun rises and sun sets in my time away from home, and they've been remarkable. But you take my breath away with your beauty."

"Did you just compare me to a sun rise?" He grinned at her, and thought that he didn't do that often enough. "You're a sap. A fucking sap that needs to have his head examined. I don't think you're seeing the overall big picture here. I'm a monster. I mean, not all the time, but that matters little in the larger scheme of things."

She looked down at the wreckage and he turned to do the same. From their vantage point, he could not only see who was down there, but could read the license plates of all of the vehicles as well. Relaying the information back to Lauren, he asked her who was in the diplomatic car that showed up, as well as asked her why they were there.

One of the dead is a man by the name of Jackson. He and the pilot were on their way to a meeting in Ohio, or so the paperwork that they turned in said. But they were armed with a great many weapons on their ride, and enough of it to have destroyed most of the downtown area. Hawk told Jamie what Lauren had said. *The diplomat, I haven't any idea who it is right now. See if your mate does, please. And be nice to her. I've yet to tell you what I've found out.*

Hawk told Jamie what Lauren needed and she nodded. When she didn't say anything, he asked her what was wrong. Jamie said that Lauren wasn't their only target, he was as well. They had been caught up in something recently—she had only just figured that out—that had stopped several shipments of arms that came in.

"The man in the limo, he's an envoy to the president. While he doesn't seem to think that the president knows about his little scheme of making deals, there is an ongoing investigation that Lauren is looking into." He asked her if they were in trouble with this. "I suppose it depends on what your idea of trouble is. They want you both dead, and your families. The man in the limo is, as we speak, trying to find out what he can about the two of you and where you live. The people there, the ones that know you, aren't saying a word to him."

Hawk told Lauren and waited while she cussed, stringing words together that didn't make any sense—but he supposed that was the point. Hawk didn't know what to think about this. If they found either of them, they'd have to be protected forever. Men like this, they'd never give up until they got what they wanted.

"Lauren knows the man. As do you. His name is Frank Jackson. He's the bastard that you've been trying to pin gun sales on for eight months. And he's right, the president doesn't know at this time about his work, but he will soon enough. Lauren needs to drop this, or she'll be hurt." Hawk told her that she'd not do that. "Yeah, I didn't think she would."

He had no idea what to do about this. The man had been in on several meetings with them. Their home addresses were only known to Jarvis and no one else. Not even a scrap of paper had them. Sitting down on the ground, he thought of what he'd been working on recently and thought of two things.

"I was to take down a man that is dealing with arms on the street. He was just under the radar until recently. Then he started selling higher priced as well as bigger weapons. I'm going to see him in two days to buy from him." Jamie told him that he wouldn't now, he had been the pilot. "Good. The other thing that I am involved with is a trail of weapons going across the states. They're dropping the load off, then someone picks it up. It's never at the same place twice so far. We can't keep an eye on them because they have monitors on their trailers, as well as the truck cabs. Also, we're waiting to catch one of them so that we can follow him back to wherever they're starting out from."

"Again, the pilot, though he wasn't the only one in charge. And the shipments won't stop until they're all dead or captured." He nodded, no longer talking to Lauren too. He asked Jamie if she had anything else for them. "Yes. I'm not going to be able to leave you like I had hoped. The men will harm you, if not destroy all that you love. I don't mean just family, though they'll be harmed as well, but the town and everyone that lives and works there. Everything."

"Thank you. I honestly don't know what to do without you helping us with the information that Lauren would eventually get, but perhaps too late." She looked at him, and he felt her sadness all the way to his heart. "I won't rush you into anything, Jamie. I might be a big hulking sort of man, but I'm not a brute or a bad person. My mom would kick my ass if I ever tried that."

"You said you have a house?" Hawk nodded. "We'll go there and figure this out. I'm going to vamp up your security around the place, and that of Lauren. But this doesn't mean that we're going to be any closer than we are now. You will see what I mean when I have to work."

"I don't care. I honestly don't care what you do or how you do it. So long as at the end of the day, everyone that I love is safe. And that would include you, Jamie." She rolled her eyes again, something that he found adorable rather than annoying as he would from someone else. "We'll go back to the office, and I'll take you to our home after that. All right?"

"No. It's not all right. None of this is."

She moved away from him and disappeared. Hawk thought that he was truly in over his head with this woman, and he found that he didn't care. It was sort of exciting. He only hoped that she would find him just as charming. Hawk decided that he might have to work on being charming a bit. Right now, he only knew how to be one thing—Army. He'd been in it for too long, and he had no idea how to woo a woman. He thought of his mom and decided to go and see her about this.

CHAPTER 3

Bea was nervous. She had heard that Hawkins had found his mate, but they had yet to meet her. Lauren had, and she said that she had a mouth on her worse than she did. That was saying a great deal. Also, that she was stronger than Jon. That scared her more than it comforted her. She looked at her husband and asked him what he was doing in her kitchen.

"I'm tasting things for you." She put her hands on her hips and glared. "You used to let me do this all the time. I don't care for being left out of the test tasting process. It hurts me all the way to my feels."

"Richard McCullough, you know that you are putting on weight. We all are. There will be no more stopping by the diner for you either. Reese told me that you were taste testing for her as well." He said that she'd needed him. "No, that's not what I heard. I heard that you show up every morning hoping for something new to taste. What am I going to do with you?"

He pulled her into his arms and hugged her. "Love me, my love. That's all I ever wanted from you. Your love and your friendship."

"Well, that's not the answer I was hoping for, but it's a good one." He laughed at her, and swatted her on the butt when she started toward the counter. "You sure are frisky. What have you been up to?"

"All our boys have mates now. That's the best thing I've heard for some time, you know?" Bea nodded at Rich. "I heard tell that she's a bit on the rough side, but has no trouble keeping Hawkins in his place. I wish I could have been there when she punched him in the face. That must have been a sight."

"I'm sure that she had a reason to do it. Lord knows that I can think of a reason hourly to do the same to you." He looked at her with a wounded expression. But beneath it, she could see the twinkle in his eyes and the mirth on his lips. "You never were one to keep your mouth shut. There are days when I swear you were hatched under a rock."

"But you love me, don't you, darling?" She told him that she did. "Good. Now, what are we having tonight to welcome the newest member to our family? By the way, did you hear that she's hanging around to help Hawkins and Lauren out? I was dumbfounded when I heard that. And here I thought that Lauren knew it all."

"She'd like for you to think that, I believe. But whatever the reason is, I'm hoping that she will stay here with him. Having Hawkins leave us again, I don't think that my heart could take that." She had lost him to the Army when he was so young. And they got to see him, but not often enough for her. And now that he was home, she found that she missed him more when he went off to work. "I wonder what sort of person this woman is. Is she nice or really as rough as you've been told? I know that she's not a pushover if Lauren likes her. Lauren would befriend a braying jackass if he was able to help her with things."

"Yeah, I think you're right about that. But I know as much as you do about her. She's a lab rat like Jon was. She's powerful, even more so than him. And she is being looked for." Rich shook his head. "You think there will ever be a time when we don't have to worry about someone coming to get one of our children?"

"Doubtful. But they all live their lives to the fullest. And we have grandchildren to fuss over and babysit. I don't think I'd have it any other way, would you?" He shook his head and smiled at her. "Now, go and set the dining room table up for all of us. I've already talked to the girls, and they're each bringing something to share. And before you ask, no, Lauren isn't bringing any Army rations. Nor, thankfully, is she cooking."

"Yeah, that is something to be thankful for. Oh, before I forget, you aren't to touch the newest daughter. Not unless she gives you permission." Bea asked him what he meant. "I don't know. I was just told not to touch her unless she gives you the okay or something. It will hurt you or her, I guess."

She was going to ask him where he'd gotten his information when her sons came home. They came en masse, and she loved it. All six of her boys under one roof again, and all of them with a wife now. Well, not Hawkins yet, but she had faith in him.

"Everyone, I'd like you to meet James Fitzpatrick. She goes by Jamie." Bea glanced at Hawkins to see if he was joking or not, but one look at him and she was happy to see that he was in love with the girl. And he was also befuddled about

35

something. "We're working things out between us, and she's thinking I'm not charming."

"I never said that, you moron. You said you were charming, and I just rolled my eyes at you. Who does that? Tells someone that they're charming?" Jamie looked around the room at them all, then looked at Bea. "You're either very brave, or simply too dumb to realize these guys will eat you out of house and home. I'm thinking brave. What do you think?"

"Well, I don't want to be considered dumb about anything. And if it's all the same to you, I'd rather you didn't start off a conversation with me calling me such." Jamie just grinned at her and she fell right in love with the girl too. "I've been told not to touch you. Is that true?"

"Yes. Unless of course you're fond of getting kicked hard in the ass." Bea laughed when the rest of them stepped back. Jamie glanced at them and then at her again. "They're afraid of me. Why is that, I wonder? Because if it's my mouth, you're really fucked regarding that. I don't change for anyone."

"Yes, it's your mouth, but I think I can overlook it if you would keep it to a minimum for me." Jamie said that she'd work on it but not to expect any miracles. "I'll take what I can get. May I hug you, dear?"

"Yes. But again, don't expect too much from that." Bea was delighted with her and wrapped her arms around the younger woman. When she pulled back and looked at her, Bea had a feeling that she was looking deep into her soul. "You don't have to worry about that. I won't leave until this is over. Your family, they'll be all right if I can make it so."

"Thank you. I guess, again, that's all I can ask for."

Bea looked at her son and went to Colin to get one of her

grandchildren. When Jamie came with her but stood back, she handed her the little girl.

She didn't know who was more surprised, Jamie or Abby. They stared at each other for a good minute or two before Abby reached out to hug her. When Jamie allowed it, Bea looked at Lauren, who held the other two babies. She seemed as surprised as Jamie did.

"Abby doesn't allow anyone to hold her but the four of us. Even her uncles can't." Jamie said nothing, but stared at the baby when Lauren spoke again. "What were the two of you doing, anyway? Talking or some shit like that?"

Bea supposed at sixteen months, they weren't considered babies any more, but she loved them all. They all seemed to be waiting for Jamie to answer when Abby laid her head on Jamie's shoulder and closed her eyes. That was something else that the little girl would not do—nap without being rocked.

"She doesn't care for the lunch that she had today." Lauren asked Jamie if she was serious. "Yes, Abby doesn't care for green beans. She's been sliding them over to her sister's plate when you're not looking. Also, she would like to be able to say the words when she wants to. I don't think she cares for mimicking you guys saying Mom or Dad."

"That's not possible." Colin glanced at Lauren when he spoke. "Is it? I mean, can she speak to our children?"

"It would appear so. Maybe you should hand her David. She could probably see why he cries all the time until he's exhausted at bedtime." Jamie just touched the little boy, who turned to look at her. "What did he say?"

"You're not going to like it, I don't think." Lauren told her probably not, but to tell her anyway. "He's afraid of the stuffed thing in his bed. Since he has no idea what it is, I can't tell you. But it scared him the way it falls over on his face and makes him afraid."

Colin laughed, and everyone turned to look at him. "The stuffed thing is a bear, believe it or not. And on more than one occasion, I've found it very close to his face. Scared me too. We'll take it out as soon as we get home. Thanks."

"No worries."

Bea watched Jamie. She was nervous, and Bea could understand that. Her sons were all large men. The women were smart and didn't take much guff either. Bea thought that she'd be nervous too if she were to be dropped in this family.

"I'd like to talk to Jon, if he's here. I have something I need to ask him."

"I'm here." Jon kissed Bea on the cheek and went to stand by Jamie. He was growing up too, she thought. Her first grandson was nearly as tall as his dad was. "Is it a private matter or can you ask me here? I can tell you now, they're not going to be happy until they figure out what we talked about. They're both nosey and intrusive."

Bea herded her family into the living room to give them privacy to talk. She was also going to have a talk with Jon about calling them intrusive. They were just a very concerned family, and needed to know things to keep them safe.

Hawk was the last to come into the room with them, but he didn't seem to be upset about Jamie needing to talk to Jon. When he sat down next to Parker, he asked him about his garden. They were talking about the induction of some kind of pesticide that was safe both for the plants and humans when Jon came in alone.

"Where did she go?" Jon put up his hand and asked Hawkins to wait until he explained something. "She's gone after those men, hasn't she?"

"Not the men you think, but yes, she's gone after two more of the idiots that are searching for her. She said to tell you that she'd not kill them if they didn't do anything stupid. That's not exactly how she said it, but you get it." Hawk grinned and nodded. "I know where she's gone, but it will do you no good to travel there to be with her. She will have it taken care of in moments."

"Then what did she want to talk to you about? I mean, if that's all, she could have said it to our faces." Bea looked at her husband when Jon did. "There's more to this than a couple of idiots chasing her, ain't there?"

"Yes." Jon looked at Hawk before he continued. "She said that she'd explain when she returned. To not hold dinner on her. I'm all for waiting for her if you guys don't mind."

Everyone agreed that they'd wait on her to return. And within a couple of minutes she was there and handed a slip of paper to Lauren. "In the event you want to look the address up, I thought this would save you time."

"Who are they? Or should I ask who were they?" Jamie asked Lauren if they could eat first, and she promised to explain after dinner. "All right. But if you don't explain it to my satisfaction, I'm going to kick your ass."

Lauren was suddenly on the ceiling. Not harmed, but just hanging there like she had stepped up to the ceiling to see what was up there. Jamie rose to be at eye level with her, but didn't touch Lauren. No one said a word.

"You should know that there is no way that you can beat me at protecting. And you aren't in a position to ever kick my ass or any other part of me." Lauren laughed. "Also, and I'm sure that you realize this all on your own, I could destroy you, immortal or not."

Lauren laughed again. It was loud and contagious. After they were both on the floor once more, Bea let out a long breath before she thought that she could take a step. Lauren asking if she could hug Jamie was comical too. Jamie stepped back and asked her if she understood what she'd just said to her.

"Oh yes. And I know now that you could. I've been doing some research on you. You were known as Test Subject Number one, weren't you?"

When Jamie nodded, Bea was confused. That was until she realized that Jamie had been in that dreadful lab with Jon. That, she thought, explained a great deal. But it also opened up as many questions as it did answers.

Bea called dinner, and as they sat down, she realized that no one cared about what Jamie had done. Least of all Lauren. This was getting stranger and stranger.

~*~

Hawk was washing the pots used to make dinner when Reese came into the kitchen with a large cake. And it was beautifully decorated too. But he had no idea who Phillip was, nor why they had his cake.

"His mom ordered it two weeks ago and said that she'd be in yesterday to pick it up. When she was a no-show, I called to ask if she was coming. She told me that she'd gone with someone else that was cheaper." Hawk asked her what she'd done about that. "Oh, I took a picture of this cake and sent it to her. She sent one of the cake she had gotten cheaper back to me. Here, have a look."

The cake was beyond ugly. Okay, he thought, perhaps it was because Reese's had been so beautiful. There were cars on the top of the other cake, while Reese had put trucks and cars on hers. The piping around the cake was blue and was set off with small signs, like stop and yield. The other cake had a handful of roses on the top and three or four around the bottom. That was not a cake made for a little boy.

"She begged me not to ban her from coming to my place. I told her that I didn't work that way, and really wished that she'd given me notice that she'd gotten a cheaper cake. The woman said she got just what she paid for and would never do that again. Want a piece of it?"

As she cut up the cake, the rest of them came into the kitchen. Ice cream was pulled out of the freezer and plates passed around to everyone. He noticed that Jamie declined a slice in favor of just ice cream. She said that she'd never cared for sweets.

Jon stood beside him as he ate his piece of the marble cake. "They would trick her into taking meds by wrapping it in sweets."

He looked at the younger man and asked him what else they'd done to her in the name of science?

"Kept her locked away from sunshine. Wouldn't feed her until she allowed them to do some experiment on her. Things that had I known about them back then, I would have taken her with me. Hawkins, you're going to have to jump through hoops for her. She has no trust for anyone. She'll help you and the family, but she doesn't trust any of you."

Instead of being angry at her for that, all Hawkins could think of was that it was sad. She was kept no better than an animal would have been—probably worse.

He went to her when she had herself plastered against the wall so no one would touch her. His cell phone rang just as he was going to ask her if she wanted to go home. It was his business phone, so he had no choice but to take the call. The first thing Jarvis, the president, said to him was congratulations.

"Thanks. What do you have for me?" Taking Jamie's hand in his, he made his way out to the back deck. It was quieter than the house, and a lot more private. "I'm assuming it has to do with the arms deals."

"Yes. I don't know how you figured it out, but I thank you for it. I'm to understand that your mate is a bit of a wizard herself. I'm assuming that she had a bit to do with it. Burcher—err, Lauren said that she was the one that found it." He told him that she had. "I'm going to owe her something for this. But for now, I need for you to come back for a few days. I've had your home cleaned, and it's been stocked too. Had I known that a mate was coming, I wouldn't have asked you to help me. Bring the mate with you, and maybe I'll get to meet her. You never know, I might impress her a little."

"Doubtful. Lauren is upset that Jamie isn't afraid of her, nor does she pay her any respect the way she thinks that Jamie should." He laughed again and watched Jamie as she walked the length of the deck and back. Not casing the joint as he might have thought, but just taking a stroll. "I'm thinking that she might be able to help me with whatever you have going on there."

"So do I." That statement alone made him stressed. "There is some shit going on here that I'm not in the loop about. Not that I'm worried about myself, but there are a great many people that work here. I don't want anyone hurt."

"I understand. I can be there in an hour. I have my family around me, and if I just take off, they'll wonder. And that's not good for any of them." Jarvis told him that he understood. "All right, we'll be there soon. I'll meet you in the normal place."

He closed his phone and watched Jamie come back to where he was standing. When she didn't say anything he just enjoyed looking at her. She was wearing a pretty blue top and a pair of jeans that he'd love to see torn from her and on the floor.

"Is sex all you ever think about?" He told her normally not, but with her, it was all he could think about. "This man you were talking to, he's a good man?"

"Yes, the best." She nodded and turned her back to him. "Did you get something from him that I need to know about? Whatever my opinion of the man is, if he's a fuck up, then he's toast."

Coming up behind her, he touched her arms then wrapped his around her. She was warm, and when she leaned back against him, Hawk could've shouted his joy to the world. But he only held her.

"The trouble that he has, do you know what it is?" He said he thought it was the arms being sold. "No. He's met a woman, and he wants you to watch her for a few days. Not that he's in love with her or anything, but he would like to be."

"What's her name, do you know?" When she pulled away from him, he didn't pout like he wanted to. Christ, he *was* a sap. "Jamie, if you know something, I'd like you to tell me."

"I need to speak to your family." He nodded and waited for her to continue. "The woman is someone I can touch because he's touched her. But what do I tell him if this woman is a double agent or something? I mean, you do know who this man is, don't you? I mean, he's the fucking president."

"I'm well aware of who he is. We're good friends, believe it or not." The door to the deck opened and he told his dad that they'd be right in. When he went back inside, Hawk turned to Jamie again. "Is that how it works for you? You have to have some sort of connection before you can tell anyone what's going on?"

"Sort of. If I can touch a person that has had some contact with someone, I can go and trace them backwards. But I can only get what the other person is thinking at the time. There isn't anything I can search for. Unless, and this is tricky, the person that I'm touching has had a great deal of contact with the other person." He stood up from the railing on the deck that he'd sat on, so he wouldn't go beg her to let him touch her. "I'm afraid that your family is not going to like me. Not that I give a fuck, but you will be upset with them should they voice it. And unless you want me to—I don't know, kick them in the ass like I think you need on occasion, I'm worried."

"I don't think that's going to happen, love. They already like you. And please don't kick my ass where my brothers, and for God's sake Lauren, can see you do it." She told him she'd think about it, then asked him how he knew that his family would like her. "My mom is the type of woman that will tell you straight up if she doesn't like you or something that you've done. And if that had been the case, you wouldn't have sat at the table with us but been standing on the outside. She likes you, so that means they all do. Not that she'd make them, but Mom has a good sense for a person and their worth."

When she moved toward the door, he followed her. Hawk was close enough to her that he could have touched her if he wanted. So, when she turned around and kissed him, he was

44

so surprised by it that he didn't kiss her back. Jamie reached for the door handle, but he pulled her back and against his body. Christ, he wanted her with a passion he'd never felt before for anything.

Pressing her against the wall didn't give him any relief, nor did it when she wrapped her legs high up on his hips. Hawkins wanted to tear her clothing off and take her right there. He knew deep in his heart that she'd never leave him after that. Or so he hoped with all his heart. But they were right outside his parents' living room, and they'd hear them. Because he had no doubt that he was going to roar when he filled her.

Pulling away from her was the hardest thing he'd ever done. Even more so than the first time he'd had to do this. Resting his forehead on hers, he laughed a little. Jamie jerked his head up.

"Ow, what was that for?" She glared at him harder. "Please tell me so that I won't be bald forever."

"You laughed at me. You fucking cock sucker, you aren't—"

To be able to explain to her, he kissed her, hungrily.

"I was laughing because of the predicament that we're in. We have started this twice now and had to pull back for one reason or the other. Actually, you left me before. Just poof and you were gone." She watched his eyes, no doubt seeing if he was lying to her. "This time we're outside my parents' home, and I'm sure as shit thinking they'll feel the house move when I take you against it."

"You're very strange. And have quite a high opinion of yourself. Why is that, I wonder?" He kissed her again and sat her down on the deck. "I want you. I don't know why, but I can't think beyond you taking me."

"Tell them what you need to tell them, and I'll take you to our house and ravage you several times before I think I'll be partially satisfied." She rolled her eyes at him again. "You're going to have to come up with another way of finding me full of shit. Rolling your eyes at me is not at all scary."

"Then how is this?" He didn't know whether to cry or laugh when she picked him up by his balls. Christ, he'd been hard before she'd touched him, and now all he wanted was for her to strip him naked and take him. "You're enjoying this, aren't you?"

"I am. Very much so. Why don't we get this over with inside, and I promise you, I'll live up to the high opinion I have of myself." She went into the house, but Hawkins stood on the deck for several minutes, smiling. He was sure that he'd not done enough of that either, smiling. Hawkins wondered whether after sex he'd be purring too.

Going inside, he noticed that everyone was in the living room. This was going to be scary, he just knew it.

CHAPTER 4

Jamie waited for Hawk to sit down. He was making her nervous the way he kept bouncing up and down. Finally she'd had enough.

"Sit the fuck down before I put you down. And that's exactly what I mean. Why are you forever moving around?" He told her that he'd been Army for too long. "Well, you won't be anything else if you don't sit your ass down and behave."

Glancing around the room, she wondered what they'd think of her when she told them some of the things she'd done to survive. Or even when she'd not been as good with the power as she was now. She looked at Bea, and she gave her a thumbs up. Jamie only hoped she'd feel that way when this was done.

"I'm a weapon. That's why the people are searching for me. And I'm controlled with it." Lauren asked her to show them. "All right, but don't touch the heat. Nor move too close to me when I'm hot. I don't want you burned."

Closing her eyes against the brightness of what she was doing, she knew the exact moment when they figured out what she was. A monster of epic proportions. When she looked at them through the haze of heat, she focused on Hawk. Jamie didn't want to see the faces of the rest of them yet.

"I can pinpoint where I want the flame to go." For an example of that, she reached out to the wood in the fireplace and set it to flame. "And when I'm done with whatever I do like this, there would be no trace of a fire, nor would anything be scorched. Not even the carpet or ground where I'm at."

"How long did it take you to learn that thing?" She looked at Rich, and was surprised that he was smiling at her. "Go on now, we're not worried about you making flaming steaks out of us."

Taking the flame back, she shifted into a cannon and dropped a ball from it. Then she became a tank, next she morphed into Rich, then Bea, all within minutes. Becoming herself again, she stood there and waited for them to tell her to get out.

"The tank, can you move like a real one or just hide that way?" She told Lauren that she could move, but since she'd never had the occasion to see one move, she didn't know how. "I'll take care of that for you if you want. I'd rather see you as a tank than in someone's lab."

Rich asked her if she could speak like him. Without shifting, she repeated his question in his own voice.

"Well, I'll be shoved into a keyhole. That's just wonderful. And if you can take out the trash when like me, I'll be beholden to you forever." Jamie looked at Hawkins, sure that he'd tell them that this wasn't normal nor anything to be happy about. "You know, I can see now why they'd want you. Not that they're ever going to touch you, but I can see it now. You don't want to be a weapon for them. Good for you."

"You're not seeing this right, damn it. I'm not only able to make a flame dance in the fireplace, but I can pull a person to me and incinerate them without anyone ever knowing." They all nodded their heads, and Mackenzie raised her hand. "This isn't a class room. You can yell out whatever you want."

"What does it do to your physical self to change into flames? Or anyone for that matter. Will we need to have an extra supply of juice or something on hand?" Jamie tried again to tell them they weren't getting it. Mackenzie smiled at her. "Oh, we're getting it just fine. I think it's you that doesn't get it. You think what? That we'd toss you out on your ass because of what you do? Not going to happen, I'm afraid. We're a family that works together and stays together. And when you ever need to become something else, then I for one would like to be prepared for what you need when it's done."

"I told you that they'd not care." Hawk stood up and came toward her. "Something that she failed to tell you about is that if you come at her with anger or the wish to keep her someplace that she doesn't want to be, that's when you get hurt, as does she. Like an imprint of the touch is on her. Touching her because you want to show her how much you love her is just fine."

"I've killed people." Hawk said that he had as well. Lauren said that she'd done it too. "I did it in order to survive. Stole things that would feed me. Don't you find any of this appalling?"

"No, my dear, we do not." Bea hugged her and smiled at her. "I'm so happy that you had the means to keep yourself safe and your belly filled. Otherwise you'd have not been here to make my son happy. And he is. For the first time in more years than I want to think about, he laughs and smiles more."

49

"You think that's because of me?" Bea nodded and said that he loved her. "No, you can't want him to be in love with me. I'm not human."

"Oh, my dear, neither are we." She started to tell her that she was a lot more than just not human, she was a monster. But Bea put her hand over her mouth. "I want you to say to me and the rest of us that you'll not just protect us, but help us any way that you can. But most importantly, I want you to love my son the way that he does you. Because as surely as I'm standing here, he'd do anything in the world to have you by his side."

She looked around the room, and Jamie could see that they were all in with what Bea had said. When Hawkins came to stand behind her, she knew that she'd lost. Or maybe she hadn't, she thought with the next breath. Having a family was an experience that she'd never had before. And she wasn't even sure how to have one.

Giving up, she repeated the words back to them all, except for the thing about Hawkins loving her. She was sure that Bea had it wrong.

"We're going home. Don't text me, message me, or call." Hawkins wrapped his arms around her and continued. "If any of you show up at my house before Friday, I will hurt you. Or have Jamie do it. Stay away."

She was in his bedroom before she could say how embarrassed she was at what he'd said. But before she could get pissed off at him and call him a few choice names, he pulled her to his body and kissed her.

Her clothing was torn from her body. The sound of it tearing and the way that Hawkins was breathing hard made her want him more. She tore at his clothing; finding him armed didn't faze her or slow her down one bit. Jamie just dropped them to the floor as she found them.

The bed behind her seemed to reach up and catch her. Hawkins was tasting her skin, nibbling at her flesh. When she could no longer stand the torture he was giving her, Jamie pulled him up by his hair again.

"I would love to hear you say my name rather than pull my scalp off." Hawkins grinned at her and she got to see his chest. Running her hand over the smooth area of him, she felt her mouth water to taste him herself. "You're making it harder and harder to take you slowly like I'd love to do."

"I thought that you'd be furred." He sat up on the side of the bed and she climbed on his lap. She told herself it was to get a better look at him, but his cock was heavenly, and she had to distract herself or come before he did. "You have well defined muscles, but no scars to speak of. I would have thought you'd been hurt some in the service."

He lifted her from his lap and lowered her over his cock. Hawkins groaned, then moaned when she adjusted herself over him. When he stopped her by putting his hands on her hips, she smiled at him.

"I'm a shifter, no scars. And the muscles are from what I was doing all the time." He kissed her throat, then pulled her closer to him. "If you ride me right now, I'll make it worth your while."

"I've had sex, but it wasn't anything like this." He said that he was glad to hear that. "What I mean is, this will be the first time I've had a vested need to see where this goes."

Hawk turned on the bed, taking her with him. When he was over her, still deep inside of her, she cried out when he cupped her ass and brought her closer. Then he moved his mouth over her breasts, teasing each of them before moving to the other. His hands were everywhere, but she wasn't getting enough. Ready to bash his head in if he didn't do something quickly, she was surprised when he stopped all movement.

"I love you, Jamie. And while I can wait until you say it back to me, I want you to know how precious you already are to me." Jamie looked into his eyes as he continued. "I'll never be able to take a breath without thinking about how much I love you and need you. My heart will not beat until I feel yours beneath my hand. My taste is attached to you. My need for you will never be sated for as long as I live without you here. I love you, Jamie. With all my being."

Pulling him down for a kiss, she moaned when he rocked into her harder, faster than before. His hands were still all over her body, but he was no longer gentle but showing her what she could expect from him. And when he commanded her to come with him, Jamie screamed out her release, knowing that this was going to be the first of many.

It felt as if he was making love to her and not her body. He was loving and needy. She was as well, but having him inside of her was something that she'd never experienced before—she could feel him. Every muscle, all the grooves of his cock. And when he cried out, she came with him. Once. Twice. Then a third time before he dropped over her.

She giggled, something that she would swear she'd never done before, and he looked down at her. After a quick kiss to her mouth, he rolled over and took her with him. He never let her go, didn't take his hands off her.

"I'm sorry that was so fast." She was sure he was joking. "I meant to make it last for hours, but when you tightened around me, it was all I could do not to pull my cock out and come all over your luscious body."

"You nearly killed me as it was. If you'd have taken that long to let me come with you, I might well have bashed your head in like I want to do a great deal when we're together." He laughed, and she laid her head down on his chest and toyed with his nipple without thought to what she was doing. "I'm not sure what to say to you now. I want to tell you how much I enjoyed that, but it sounds lame."

"No, tell me how magnificent I was." She looked at him again. "If you keep playing with me like that, I'm going to take you again. This time I will make you suffer."

Jamie had it hit her all at once. She loved him. Her heart skipped several beats while she tried to convince herself it was just the sex, but it didn't work. She was in love with the man. Not wanting to look at him when she told him, Jamie put her hands on the bed so that she could flee if need be. Yes, he'd said it first, but he might have been wanting to get laid. Jamie knew that to be untrue the moment she thought it.

"I've never loved anyone before. Not in all my life did I ever understand the feelings that were involved in it. It's consuming, isn't it?" He lifted her chin up and stared at her. "I'm in love with you, Hawkins. I don't know how it happened, but if you were telling me a fib before, about loving me, I'll understand. It was just hormones."

This kiss was different than any other kiss he'd given her. It was as consuming as his love was. Hawkins made love to her mouth as he had her body, leaving no part of it without his taste. And when he lifted his body enough from hers that she could touch him, Jamie explored him as he was her.

~*~

Hawkins couldn't get enough of her. Not just making love

to her, but herself too. Their love making now had turned into giving the other satisfaction. What Jamie didn't know, but he would tell her, was that he'd never been more satisfied than he was right here in her arms.

"Hawkins, please. I'm drowning in need for you." He told her to say it again. And when she looked into his face, he felt the overwhelming emotion of it. "I love you, Hawkins McCullough."

There wasn't any holding back for either of them. Hawkins came twice, his body covered in sweat from trying to hold back for her. Jamie screamed several times, her body bowing up off the bed with each release. Her nails raked over his back until he felt the blood moving over his skin. Then when he thought that he was finished, that he couldn't come again, she tightened around him again and he came hard enough to make him weak with it.

This time when he dropped over her, he couldn't move. If someone came for them, they'd both be taken. When she pushed him off her he groaned loudly, his body protesting even the smallest movement of his head adjusting to the pillow.

When Hawkins woke he was alone in the big bed. The place where she'd been each time he opened his eyes was still warm from her body. Hawkins sat on the side of the bed and tried to reason with his feet that they could indeed handle his weight. They, too, wanted to go back to the warm bed.

Forcing his body to do what he was telling it, he made his staggering way into the bathroom. Looking in the mirror, Hawk could see the man that Jamie had made him.

His face wasn't tense like it usually was. There were lines around his eyes, not from straining to see what he could kill, but from laughter. The pinched look of his mouth was gone, and he looked relaxed and even formed a genuine smile. Turning on the water to clean up, he reached for Jamie and found her in the kitchen with Jarvis.

Then it hit him. He was supposed to go to Washington last night and bring Jamie with him. Hurrying through his shower now, he was combing his hair when he realized that he no longer wanted to do this. No more hunting and killing. Making his way down the long staircase, Hawkins was ready to tell Jarvis that he quit when he saw the man.

"What the fuck happened to you?" He examined the cuts on Jarvis's face and those on his arms. "What did you do, get into a fight with a rose bush? Where else are you hurt?"

"See, I told you that he loved me like a father." Jarvis looked at him and smiled. "I'm all right. Your lovely mate here gave me the once over too, and was much harsher about asking me what I'd been up to. If you would call for Lauren and Colin, I'd like to say this only one time."

In the time it took for Lauren and Colin to get to his home, Jamie and he were making breakfast. Hawkins lived by the rule that the first meal of the day set the tone for the entire day. He was fucked if that were really true. He not only burned the toast, but he'd forgot to put baking soda in the biscuits before baking them.

"Those look like something that I'd cook." Lauren took the offered plate of ham and eggs. There was toast too. "Come on, big boy, let's get this over with so we can fix it for him. With the four of us working together, we can do this in no time."

"Four?" Jamie shook her head even as Lauren was nodding at her. "I'm not a part of whatever you have going on with this. Hell, I don't even understand half of what he told me when he got here. Something about a convoy and men taking advantage of a wrecked car."

"My dear girl, you should have asked me to explain it to you. But I told you that I was in a convoy, and that when they rammed my car from behind, I was hurt that way." Lauren asked Jarvis where this had happened. "Near here. I can take you there if you'd like."

"No need. Mac and Jamie can get there before we could even get in the car."

Hawk held her hand as she touched her fingers to Jarvis's head. When they were near the accident a few seconds later, she could see that it had been an ambush, not a regular accident.

"They're cleaning it up. And without alerting the police, I think." Hawk started down the hill, and he was glad when she followed. Almost as soon as they were seen, Jamie took the form of Lauren, and it became apparent that they knew who she was.

"What the holy fuck are you doing? Don't you know this is my crime scene? Who's your superior that has you guys mopping up this fucking mess without me being here?" He watched the four men and had to really bite his lip hard when they nearly wet themselves to get her answers. "Well, dog face, what is going on here?"

The first man told her everything. How they had been sent to ram the limo that was coming across their paths. "But I swear to you, sir...ma'am...I swear to you that we none of us knew what we were into until it was too late." She asked him who was the dead man—because he would be soon—that sent them. "Jackson, ma'am. He not only sent us here, but he said that we were to shoot all the survivors if there were any. I wasn't going to shoot the president. No way, no how."

"Oh, I see. You would have shot anyone else that might have been in it, though. If you tell me yes, I'm going to take your head off at the neck." He said that they'd been ordered to do it. "This Jackson person, is he Army, Navy, or some other form of service that you've heard of? He's not, just so you know. And from what I know of him, he's nothing but a fucking civilian. What the fuck are you doing taking orders from a fucking civilian?"

She ordered them to get on their knees with their hands above their heads. None of them had an answer to her query. When she pulled out her gun, Hawk thought for sure she was going to kill them all. And when she put the gun to the first man that had spoken to her, he nearly leapt at her to stop.

"Is this what you would have done if a person came out of that limo you wrecked to fuck? What if it had been little Tommy Jones, treating his nice new girlfriend to a little trip in a limo? One that he'd been saving up for, for months?" The man said he'd not thought of that, he was following orders. "Orders that you had no business whatsoever in following in the fucking first place. Christ almighty, you just tried to kill the fucking President of the United States. Do you have any idea what is going to happen to you now? You are done, that's what you are. Make up your wills, boys, you're going before a firing squad."

The man with the gun to his head started crying. Jamie/Lauren seemed at a loss as to what to do now. Hawk stepped up to the man at the end of the line and shot him in his leg. That got their attention right away.

"Go over there and sit on the side of the road. Maybe, if

you're lucky, a car will come around the corner and fucking kill you all. It'll be better treatment then what you'll get when you're arrested." Hawk winked at his mate and watched her seem to back off.

He heard the car then and told Colin and Lauren to stay put. He didn't need the real Lauren coming up there now. *We have it covered. Well, Jamie does. She looks like Lauren, and even sounds like her when she's trying to make a point. And she certainly has her vocabulary down pat.*

I told Lauren, and she wants me to come there and see what she looks like and sounds like. This is epic — you know that, don't you? Christ, the things she could do for people is amazing. I mean, think of being able to have a double when you just can't make a meeting. Not for bad things, never that, but this is cool. I'm coming up.

When his brother got there, he had to take a second, then a third look. He asked her if she needed him and Jamie nodded.

"I want you to gather up these fucking shit heads and call for someone to come and pick them up. No, wait." She looked at the man that she'd been fucking with. "No, we need them to tell Jackson that it's done. That they killed all the survivors."

"How do we do that? It's doubtful they're going to do anything for us. They're about to shit themselves now, they're so afraid of you. Or Lauren." Hawk smiled at her. "I think you're sexy."

"Are you fucking insane? You have to be." Jamie started stomping away, mumbling to herself about shit heads and fucking idiots. He wasn't sure which category that he fit in, but he was having fun working, and that was a first for him. He looked at his brother when he laughed.

"I have no idea what she's done to you, but I'm really glad she did it." Hawk told Colin that she loved him and he her. "Yeah, I can see that too. But it's not only that. You're more the way you used to be when we were younger. Before you started hiding away from us all."

"I was. I guess you could say that I've been waiting for her to come to me my whole life. I can't believe that I put up such a fuss about all this. And you know what, Colin? She makes me feel as if I'd like to live forever instead of just having it given to me." Colin nodded and hugged his brother. "Now, I have to go see if she's calmed enough to tell me what we're doing. She has a very devious mind too."

Colin was still laughing as he made his way back to Lauren, the real one this time. And Hawk made his way to the four men and his mate. She was asking them how they were to contact this Jackson person. Of course. none of them were talking. Hawk reached out and touched the first man.

"Benson is supposed to contact Jackson. But this fucktard has no idea what he's supposed to say." Hawk touched the next man. He wasn't gentle when he raped his mind, but he found out which one was Benson. It was the guy that had had the gun to his head. "Your favorite boy has it all."

When Jamie touched the man's head, he screamed. She apparently wasn't being gentle either. And when the man fell over, Jamie looked at him. He knew in that moment that this had gone to fuck in a heartbeat.

"We need to go. Now. Tell your Colin and Lauren to get the fuck out of here. They're coming for them." Hawk ran for the hill they'd come from right behind Jamie. Telling his brother to get out, he heard the helicopter coming in. From the sound of it, he'd say it was heavy. Armed well. "Hurry. We don't want to be here."

They were flat on the ground when someone in the

helicopter opened fire on the four men. If they thought it was strange that they were sitting there with their hands on their heads, he didn't care. But this shit had just gotten real. He asked Colin if they were all right after making sure that Jamie was.

"Yeah, we had passed an open barn on the way here and I'm inside it. Christ, what the fuck was that? And how the hell did she know that they were going to kill them?" He told him he didn't know but he'd say they were lucky she'd been there. "Yeah, no shit. We'd be alive, but in fucking bad shape. Now what do we do?"

"Lay low? I haven't any idea. Let me talk to Jamie." He asked again if she was all right. "What do we do now? I mean, we can move back to the house, but I think you have a plan."

"No, not really. I just...fuck they were going to kill us. What the hell is this world coming to when a girl can't just stand on the side of the road with a gun to someone's head and not be shot to fuck?" Hawkins laughed. It felt good after all the tension of the last few minutes. "Ask the real Lauren. I'm not sure I want to be her anymore."

"You saved us, love. That's all that matters now."

He reached out to his brother again and he said they needed to regroup at home. After telling Jamie what they were doing, he pulled her into his arms as they laid there and simply held her. Christ, this was as bad as it was sometimes in the service.

CHAPTER 5

Lauren paced the big office. She'd been here for an hour since the helicopter had come by, and she couldn't focus on anything but how close they'd been to being hurt. It was scary and pissed her off, but it was Jamie she was worried about.

Since they'd been back, she'd been sitting on the couch in the living room and staring at nothing at all. Lauren wanted to go in there and shake her up a bit, maybe slap her around, but every time she asked if she was all right, Hawk said that she said she was.

"Bullshit." Going to the living room where she was, Lauren stopped and watched the woman. She was crying. And it hurt her in ways that she'd never felt before. Her plan to rough her up a bit flew out the window when she sat beside her on the couch. "What's up?"

"I'm okay." Lauren snorted and said that she was not okay. "Those men are dead. And while they were going to kill the president, they had no idea what was coming at them until it was too late. I should have warned them too."

"Fuck that shit. You might have warned them, but they

would still be dead. The simple fact that they tried to kill Jarvis really would have had them in prison for a very long time. However, I've been around enough to know that they wouldn't have lasted a month in there. They would have been killed, well, by someone like me or Hawk." Jamie looked at her then. "And they were willing to kill whoever came out of that limo no matter who it might have been. Think of it this way—little Tommy's mom would have been heartbroken and have no answers."

She sat there for a few more minutes, and Lauren was ready to ask her what was wrong now. But when she looked at her, she knew that she had more information than Lauren had on this.

"The man that planned this is the one that pulled the trigger today." Her voice was soft, and Lauren asked her who it was in the same quiet way. "Jackson. Just as you think it was. But he's not finished yet. He doesn't know that the president isn't dead, but he's assuming that this would amass him a fortune. I don't know how that is supposed to happen. And he has a couple of loads of guns going out tomorrow night."

"How did you get that? I mean, I love it, but tell me how you were able to know about the helicopter and this information." She told her, and Lauren sat back on the couch as she tried to work it out in her own head. "So, because this guy that was killed today had contact with Jackson, then you could work back to him and read his mind. That's some fucked up shit you got going on there. It's like a puzzle that has those lines in it that you have to find which one gets you to the treasure."

"Yes, but I can only get whatever he's thinking about at the time. Unless I can touch him. Then I get whatever I want." Lauren thought about that. She knew that Hawk could read minds too, but he had to touch the person to get it. Even Jon could do it, but as far as she knew, he couldn't track backwards on one person to get to another one. "What is it you're thinking? By the way, being you back there, that is scary as shit the way you work. I got what I could from you and Hawk on how you'd do it if you were there."

"From what I heard, you had me dead on. Thanks for taking that on. I might well have shot the lot of them." She grinned at her. "I want you to touch Jarvis's mind. And backtrack him to Jackson. Maybe we can pick up on more of him since I'm sure that he'll be thinking of his end game."

"You want me to go into the most powerful man in the world's brain? You're as fucking nuts as Hawkins is. No way am I— What if I find out something important? Like, I don't know, the combination to the football thing that someone carries around for him?" Lauren told her. "You'd shoot me? Are you kidding? You'd shoot me if I did that? You're aware that I can murder you without anyone knowing about it, right?"

"No, I'd not do that. But it was fun seeing you all worried and shit. But the other thing, the fire? I might have a use for that later. I'm thinking that this Jackson guy isn't long for this world." Jamie asked her if she had a plan. "It'll depend on what you can find out when you search back to him. Shit, I wish you could have touched him at some point. This would have been so much better."

Lauren got up and started for the family room that she knew Jarvis was in. Boyd had come over earlier and checked out his wounds. He'd required a couple of stitches, but he was otherwise all right. Lauren turned when Jamie didn't follow her.

"You have the mind of something evil, you know that, don't you?" Lauren thanked her. "I didn't mean for you to take that as a compliment, dumb ass. I was insulting you."

"Yeah, well, I take it where I can get it. And this is the most fun I've had in a while." She told Jamie to come on. "When we get in there, it would be awesome if you were me. I like to get his panties in a twist once in a while too. Keeps him on his toes."

Having someone like Jamie to work with was great. She wished that she'd been in the service with her, and wondered what sort of messes the two of them could have gotten into. Lauren loved all the women in this family—they had all been great additions to the McCulloughs, but with Jamie, she had someone that could think like she did—on her feet—and act without hesitation. That shit got you killed if you didn't do whatever you needed when you needed.

Jarvis was, of course, willing to help out. He did caution Jamie about some of the more sensitive things that he had on his mind. She promised him that she'd only find his connection to Jackson. When he told her he was ready, Lauren asked if she could record it all. So she'd not miss anything.

"It's doubtful that she ever misses anything, my girl here. And the fact that I owe her and Hawkins my life isn't even nearly what I owe them both. They've always been there for me and this presidency." He looked at Jamie like he was going to have a fucking test later. "You, I think, are going to be on that very short list of people as well. Also, while you're in there, could you look at a woman I'm sort of seeing? And yes, I've had some contact with her, but not sexually. Just so you know going in."

"Thanks for dishing out way too much information, but all I need is her name." After he tells Jamie, Lauren is surprised as she'd thought it was someone on staff. "I can find out anything about her, but again, it might not be something you want to hear. All right?"

"Anything is better than me getting my ass handed to me if she's only out for something I don't want her to have." Lauren wanted to ask Jarvis what sort of things he thought she wanted, but didn't. Jamie was ready to start. "Now, this won't hurt at all. I'll be gentle with you. Nor do you have to think about anything in particular. I'll find it."

As Jamie sat down, Lauren thought that she'd have to keep holding his head or some shit. But once they shook hands, she just sat there drinking her glass of tea that had been set in front of her. Lauren thought it was sort of boring watching the two of them sit there until Jamie started talking.

"The woman is forefront in your mind, so let me look at her so that we can move on. Iris Nash is a divorced woman with two kids. They're doing well financially, better than well now. She's not anyone you should be seeing, I'm afraid. It's Jackson again. He's asked her to spy on you, and she's being well funded. In a few months, she is going to say that you impregnated her." Jamie paused and sipped more of her tea. Lauren had never been patient, and now wasn't any different. "She's never been in your bedroom and needs badly to get in there. Iris will be able to tell them what the room looks like, and that will be all the proof that they need to have a scandal attached to your name."

"Well fuck." They both looked at Jarvis and he laughed. "Burcher, I do believe that you're rubbing off on me. I'll end it today when I return. Thank you, Jamie. I'm indebted to you."

65

"No, that was easy. Now I need to find out about Jackson." She was quiet again, and this time Lauren had something to occupy her mind. She was going to have to help him end this with Iris. She didn't know how yet, but she would make sure that she understood not to fuck with Jarvis again. "Jackson has been in your office a great deal over the last few weeks. He is frustrated with you because you are very good at keeping your desk cleared of anything that he can use. Just this morning he was sitting in your chair, thinking about himself being there. But he won't be. He has other people that he wants in place there so that he can manipulate them, and the shit doesn't come back on him. Christ, he's a piece of work."

Jamie paused for a few moments, and Lauren thought that was all she was going to get. But when she looked at her, the hair on the back of her neck danced and her heart started to race. She asked her what she'd found.

"He, as you have probably surmised, wants you and Hawkins dead. He thinks that once you are gone, no one will be around to look into anything that he's up to. He believes that the two of you are responsible for too many things that have happened to his predecessors. And he's up to a great many things." Jamie listed off about ten things Jackson was doing to put himself in the big league of bad guys, including the gun running, which she knew about. But the money laundering for some of the biggest names on the FBI wanted list was a surprise to her. "He's dangling a carrot tomorrow, he thinks, for you to get your fucking asses dead. His words, not mine. There will be a call from the vice president, which I'm going to help him with to expedite this shit. It'll be about a terrorist coming into the U.S. VP Bentley will call for you, because that's what I'll tell him to do, and you'll be one of the many killed. He believes as of right now that Jarvis is dead."

"Can we use that?" Jarvis looked at the doorway and she turned to find Hawk there. She asked him if he needed to be brought up to date. "No. This is another one of those freaky things. I can feel and see what she does when she's searching. I was having a nice talk with Mom and Dad, and suddenly I'm in the mind of a woman I don't know."

Jamie seemed to relax when Hawk sat beside her. Lauren hadn't thought of how much this was stressing her out. Fuck, if she could do this, she'd be all over everyone's mind and not give a good fuck if they liked it or not. But Jamie, while a kick ass woman who didn't take shit, even from her, might feel like she was invading someone's privacy.

"I think that not only can we use this, but I think we can actually make it work out for a great many people. Jamie, when you were in the mind of Iris, was she being blackmailed into doing this or she was all for it?" She said she was all in. "Figures. Okay, I'll need a minute here."

Lauren went to her office and sat in her chair. This had to work out, and she'd make it work for everyone on her side. Hawk came in a few minutes later and sat in the chair across from her.

"Just like old times?" He smiled and nodded. "Okay, I'll bounce, and you tell me the million and one ways that it's not going to work, and I'll show you how it will."

"Yes. But, if you remember correctly, they all didn't usually work out." She nodded this time. "Once I said it wouldn't work, you'd try and prove to me that it would and find out I was right."

"Yeah, but don't tell Colin. He thinks I'm brilliant at figuring things out." She looked at him closely and noticed something that she'd never seen on his face before. "You're happy, aren't you? I mean, like a cone dipped in that colorful shit that looks like puke to me, kind of happy."

"Yes." Hawk laughed hard before continuing. "You know, you have such a way with showing your feelings that I'm surprised that you don't work for a greeting card company. You'd be a hit."

"Yeah?" He told her no, he'd been making a joke. "Oh. I was thinking of one that I could write up. 'Love me or leave me, I don't give a shit. So long as you don't take my dog.'"

Hawk was still smiling when she started thinking of a way to use their information. She had never seen him smile this much. And that was another thing that she'd never seen before. Hawk's laughter. Lauren thought that love did make a difference in a life. Who knew?

~*~

Hawk made his way quietly through the outer office and into the Oval Office from the door that Jarvis had given him a key to. No one was in here this late at night, so he took full advantage of the opportunity to do what he'd been sent there to do. Jarvis had also given him the key to his desk drawers, as well as the combination to the safe. He pulled out the paperwork that went into the safe just as Jamie contacted him.

I want you to know that this covert shit is for the birds. That's just my opinion. I know that it's important, but having you gone in the middle of the night isn't my idea of fun and relaxation. I want you here. He laughed as he decided which drawer the papers should be in, so anyone could find them. *Also, you should know that I'm nuts about you. Even though you're a big shithead that's never around when I need you to be.*

Oh, really? Before I left you tonight, to go on a mission that you

68

helped with, I thought for sure you were sated. You told me several times, as a matter of fact, that I wore you out and that you might not move for the rest of the night.

Yes, you did. But that's not what I need you for. Although, now that you mention it, I have recovered, and if you do whatever it is that your —

He paused in opening the drawer on the desk, and tensed up when he saw the lights go on under the door.

Don't move. He said that he wasn't planning to. *It's Jackson. He's coming in there to find something on the president. He does think that he's dead, and wonders why the police or anyone else hasn't made it public. Hide. He'll open the door, but he's going to wait to see if anyone calls out to him.*

Hawk moved back away from the desk after planting the paperwork, then made himself move to stand just outside the office. It was then that he realized too late that he'd left the drawer slightly ajar. Maybe it would be good — at least he hoped so. He pulled out his phone to start recording. The guards there couldn't see him, so he wasn't worried about being caught.

The man was about as stealthy as a child in a room full of toys. Then Hawk got to thinking about children, and wondered if Jamie would even want any with him. He wouldn't if he were her. While he was feeling a good deal better, he knew that he wasn't right in the head most —

Do you want me to come there and kick your ass? I will, damn it. Where the fuck do you get off telling me that I don't want children with you?

He told her that he'd technically not told her anything, but smiled when she put together a string of curse words that would have had Lauren impressed. *Honey, what is a fucking*

69

douche cock sucker? He laughed when she called him a dick head once again. *Your threats aren't really making me afraid of you. But I appreciate you putting me on the right path. Again.*

You just wait until you get home. I'm going to teach you the real meaning of kick your ass. You cannot be thinking that way. Not anymore. She was screaming at him in his head, and all he could do was smile. *I have had it up to here with you thinking bad thoughts. Do you hear me, Hawkins? I'm going to hurt you.*

I dearly love you, Jamie, but I'm sort of working here. You can beat me up when I get back there. She said that he could count on it. *Okay, now back to work. Jackson is taking the bait. And now he's at the safe. It seems our little Miss Iris has been very busy of late. I wonder how she found out the combination to the safe when it's not written down. Can you look, Jamie? I'm not nearly as good at this as you are. I think I only got this information because you had it from him.*

It's much too late for you to start sucking up. Let me see. Oh, and this one is all on Jarvis. He didn't change the combination from when the other guy, I think it was Joe Irwin, was there. Iris went in one day and opened it with the old combo from Irwin. She knew it from when he was there because he would have her put things in it for him. She asked if she should tell Lauren.

Not yet. I want to see what he's going to do now that he has the goods. And Jackson was working hard at getting in the safe, as he was having to start over several times before he finally got it open. *This guy is a moron, just in case you didn't know.*

Frank Jackson was going to prison, for a very long time, and Hawk was going to see to that. Just as he and Lauren had made sure that the former President Joe Irwin and Brigadier General Garth Wilson had. So, when Jackson sat in the big chair, he watched him swing around and around while Hawk recorded him acting stupid. And the way that they were going to catch him was with all the paperwork that he now had.

Jarvis had come up with that idea. Lauren had pouted for about a minute before she asked how the papers should appear. She danced around the room when Jarvis told her to make it look good. Hawk even signed his name to the documents just for the hell of it. If Jackson had been any kind of thief, he might have checked that out first. But he wasn't, and Hawk was glad for that.

In ten minutes Jackson was gone. He left behind enough prints and bodily fluids when he had sneezed all over the desk that they could convict him now. Having the cleaning crew come in late tonight to scrub the place down had done that for them. It was going to look very badly for him in the very near future.

When the door closed behind Jackson, Hawk stood there for several minutes and thought that it had been too easy. There was something about this that didn't ring true. Going back into the office, he reached out in the room, looking for anything that might be out of place, or if he'd missed something earlier. Then he found it.

I'm fucked. Jamie asked him what was going on. *There is a camera in here that recorded me in the office before Jackson. I have to trace it back to the source or he'll use it against us when we bring him in.*

Taking the camera off the corner where it had been planted, he wondered why he'd gotten in and out with the camera running. He hadn't. Since Jackson was the one that was in charge of this, then he'd be the only one that could turn it off when he was in here. Talking to Jamie, he started spit balling.

He has the room being recorded. Which is, I'm happy to say, against the law. So that means he has it running around here, and close enough where he can turn it off and on at a whim. The device that he used is high grade stuff and has a serial number on it that I'll have Lauren check. Hawk looked up at the wall where it had been and saw that a very small wire that was still there. *I'm going to try something here. I'm going to use our little power to see if I can trace this to the source.*

I can do that. Hawk did a little jig. *Okay, I don't know what you're doing right now, but you suddenly got very happy. What are you doing right now?*

Dancing. And if you tell anyone about this, I'll never let you come again. She promised him that she'd not do that. *All right, my dear, find the computer that this is feeding to.*

Got it.

Hawk had no idea why, but he'd thought it would take longer than that. When she told him where it was, he actually laughed out loud. Not only was Jackson terrible at sneaking into a room, but he was a moron at hiding things too. Hawk went to take care of it.

The computer that it was attached to was the one that Iris used. Going to the computer, he wondered what her password might be and opened the drawer. When there was nothing there, he turned over the small plastic flower that sat on her desk and found it. Some people were just too predictable. Plugging in the information, he looked for the icon for the recorder on the hundred or so icons she had on her desktop, most of which were games and shopping places. He might need to have that checked out on her usage as well.

Once he had all that he needed to turn the camera off and delete tonight's information, he decided to look for more video. Apparently this wasn't the first time that Jackson had been in the room.

Twice he'd had sex with Iris on the desk. And another time he'd had someone that Hawk didn't know. As he searched through the recordings, he set up the computer to send all the videos to his computer at home, as well as Jarvis's personal computer. He had no idea what he could use them for, but to have them was a good idea. Then he cloned Iris's computer.

What the fucking Sam hell are you doing? He smiled when he heard from Lauren. He hadn't realized that it had gotten so late, and he needed to get out before the crew came in for the day shift. Hawk told her what he was doing. He added her address to the email and sent it to her as well, and told her to look at it. *So, our little liar has been busy, hasn't he? Christ, is that Iris that he's fucking on the presidential desk? What the hell? That's some fucked up information, don't you think?*

Yes. And I've cloned her computer to set up with the one in your office. If and when – because you know that they will – they set this up again, we'll know the precise moment that she has access to it. She told him good thinking. *Also, Jamie has been helping me with this since I got here. I would have been caught without her help.*

Are you telling me that I should hire her? He told her that he'd never tell her to do anything. *No, you'd be slick about it. But I've already put the paperwork through to get her onboard and paid. She'll be behind the scenes as much as I can make it. The two of you working this way will be beneficial to a lot of people.*

I'm quitting. Hawk waited for her explosion as he left the building the same way he'd come in. When he was nearing his car, he saw Jon waiting for him. *I can't do this anymore, Lauren. It's not how I want to be a mate to Jamie.*

73

Do you think I can talk you into one more mission? It has to do with Jamie and the people searching for her. He said that he'd help with that anyway. *I know. But Christ, Hawk, what am I going to do without you there at my side?*

Raise your children and have a good long life with my brother. I'm planning to have a bunch of little Jamies and Hawks, and have a good time watching them grow up. And not have to think about where I'm going to be heading the next morning. It's got to end sometime, and I'd rather me be the one that decides when and how. Jon hugged him, and they got into his car. Before they drove off, Hawk told him that he was talking to Lauren. *Are you there?*

Yes, I'm thinking you might be right. I'm getting too old for this shit, and I've missed one of my daughters taking her first steps. He didn't point out that was what he was talking about. She'd get it sooner or later. *I'm going to think on this for a bit. But we need to finish this with Jackson. All right?*

He told her he was going to finish this with her and she seemed satisfied. When they closed their connection, he looked at his nephew. There was usually something so calming about him, but today he was tense. Before starting the car, he asked him what was going on.

"The person that is looking for Jamie is someone that I didn't expect." He asked him who it was. "Her father."

CHAPTER 6

Jarvis was sort of nervous about this morning. He was hurt, yes, but not nearly as bad as it could have been. Lauren told him to just act like nothing at all happened out of the ordinary and go on with his day. The moment that Iris walked into his office, he could tell that she was shocked to see him there.

"Sir?" He asked her what she needed. "I don't know. I mean, I didn't expect you in today at all. We heard about the accident."

There had been no report on the accident. It had been cleaned up by the McCullough family, the limo had been put in the barn, and the dead men were all in the morgue with tags on their toes that said unknown. But the look on her face was just the reaction that he had expected.

"Accident? What accident would that be?" Iris seemed unsure where to go with it, so she asked him if he was free for dinner tonight. "No, I've got a great deal on my plate right now. I'm not even sure that we should be seeing one another anymore. I've given it some thought, and I think—"

"You have to see me." Jarvis cocked a brow at her and said nothing. "What I mean is, we have such a good time when we're together. I thought we'd have dinner in your suite and then watch some television or something. Why don't we do that, and if you still think we shouldn't see each other, I'll understand."

"No. I don't think so. As I said, I'm very busy, and I just don't think this is going to go anywhere between us. I mean, from the start we both agreed that it was just a fling. And it isn't as if we made any kind of commitment to each other. It was just a meeting between two friends." He smiled at her, and it was the hardest thing he'd ever done. "We can still be friends, but not see each other outside of the office, don't you think?"

"Yes, I guess so." She looked torn, and he asked her what she needed from him. "Oh, nothing. I guess, with the accident and all, I thought I would clear your calendar for you. I'm afraid that I've lost it off my computer."

"I'll see what I can do about getting it restored to you." Jarvis lowered his head to look at the papers in front of him without really seeing them. "If there is nothing else, Miss Nash, I really need to get to work."

When the door closed behind her, he let out a long breath. He'd have to call Lauren and let her know what had happened, but right now he had to calm himself. Jarvis was the leader of the free world, and right now he thought he'd rather be in the war room making decisions than have to deal with this woman. When his phone rang, it took him several seconds to realize it was his personal phone and not the ones on his desk.

"Hey, how's it going?" Hawk. The man had a way about him lately that made him feel secure. Not that he'd ever not been there when he needed him, but he felt like he was more human lately and less like a killing machine. "I have your computer hooked up to the one here at Lauren's office. See the little icon at the bottom left? That's on a different server than you have in the White House. You can chat with any of us without letting anyone know about it. Jon set it up for us."

"Do I tell you about my morning on it? Or on the phone you called me on?" He told him he could talk on the phone, though he'd be leery about it. But the chat was clean. "I'll use that then. Are you guys going by some secret names or something? Very covert?"

Hawk laughed. "Nah, just Hawk and Lauren. Jamie might come on there too, but she'll be using mine. By the way, you should know that Lauren is going to make it public about the records in a few days. She said that she has a few friends that will take care that it's out there." Jarvis asked if there was anything that he should say. "I'd keep it low. Lauren said that you should simply say that it's an ongoing investigation and that you cannot comment at this time. It'll piss a few people off, but you'll be able to give them an answer."

"I like that. It's like I'm admitting that I know and that I'm clueless as to what is going on." Jarvis laughed, telling him what happened this morning with Iris. "I don't know what she was coming in here to do, but she was startled stupid when she saw me sitting at my desk."

"She's called Jackson already, Lauren said. She's having those conversations recorded as well. Just to cover your ass. Oh, the car is going to be dismantled. Ben, the guy that has it in his barn, said that he'd use the parts for some other cars he's been working on." Jarvis didn't care so long as it didn't come back to bite anyone in the ass. "Jackson and Iris both have trackers on their cars, so we'll be able to see where they go. I have a feeling that they're going to go to the site where you were hurt and look around. At least I'm betting Jackson will. I'll be close enough that I can see him, but him not see me. Do you have any questions?"

"Yes. When is this going to end?" Hawk asked him what he meant. "This conspiracy and crap going on. The way that I have to keep you here most of the time to cover my ass. And for that matter, why are people after my ass? I'm a good man. I think a good leader as well. When will all this just stop so I can help the country without worrying I'm going to get shot?"

"It won't." He should have known that Hawk would give him a straight up answer. No sugar coating it with that man. "I can tell you this, however. When you are no longer president, it won't be much different than it is now. Only it'll be on someone else's plate. And I'm retiring."

"I'm sorry, what did you just say?" Hawk repeated himself, and even laughed a little. "You can't retire. The country needs you and Lauren to keep us straight. What the hell will I do without you in my corner?"

"Write a book? Become a best seller and spill most of your secrets? Other than the Secret Service following you around all the time, you'll be a free man. Maybe you can find someone that you can spend the rest of your life with." He had thought that he'd had that with Iris. However, he wasn't too upset that it hadn't panned out. "However, you let us vet her for you."

He was still laughing when Hawk said that he needed to get going before Jackson got there. When he put the phone in his front jacket pocket he sat back at his desk. It wasn't as if he had nothing to do today—there was a long list of things. And now that he held his calendar close to his vest, so to speak, he'd have to remind himself when he had to leave and such.

Jarvis was just putting one of the files that he'd been working on back in the filing cabinet when his door opened. While he knew Jackson, he didn't recognize this version of him. He was unkept and hadn't shaved, it looked like. His shirt was misbuttoned like he'd just thrown it on as he was running out the door. Jarvis asked him if he was all right and had him sit down.

"There is too much going on around here." He asked him what he meant by that. "I don't know. I'm just stressed about some things. Nothing to do with you, however."

"I should hope not." Jarvis sat back down at his desk and looked at the man in front of him. He had never really trusted Jackson. And had never invited him to come into his office like he owned the place. But for now, he'd let him hang himself. "Iris and I have called it quits. We're not suited to each other, I don't think."

"What the fuck are you talking about? Iris is perfect for you." He seemed to realize that he had shouted at him and cleared his throat before speaking again. "What I mean is, Iris has made you a very happy man, hasn't she? I mean, didn't you guys have dinner up in your suite a great deal?"

"No, never. Why would you think that?" Jackson just mumbled something about nothing going right. "I'm sorry. What's not going right for you, Frank? I thought that you had all your plans all laid out and most of them executed."

Jackson just stared at him then turned to look behind him. Jarvis pretended not to notice that he was looking at the spot where the camera had been found. Jarvis wished now that he'd had some kind of recording device of his own. But that would be as bad as this man, breaking the law by recording him.

"Have you had your office scanned lately?" Jarvis said that it was scanned every day, sometimes twice. "Really? That often? I had no idea. I was curious, you see. Nothing to do with you."

"You've said that to me two times, Frank. It makes me think that something is going on that does have to do with me." Frank stood up then sat down again. There was something seriously wrong with this man if he thought that he'd get away with this. "Iris asked me about an accident yesterday."

Frank's face literally lost all color. Even his lips had gone a chalky white. Leaning back in his chair, Jarvis watched the man as he explained, as he had to her, that he'd not had one at all. Did he know what she might be referring to?

"Iris told you that? Well, you know how women can be. Maybe she said that to get you to comfort her or something." Jarvis told him that she'd said that before he'd informed her they weren't going to be together any longer. "I don't know then. I just don't know about anything of late. Have you seen McCullough or Burcher lately? I was trying to get in touch with them to ask about some projects I have going on."

Jarvis reached under his desk and pushed the button to bring security to him. They would enter and escort him out, but they'd never say a word to the man. When the door opened, Jarvis told him that he had a great deal of work to do today and that he should be on his way.

"And Frank?" He turned and looked at him with a questioning look. "Do not come into my office again without permission. I will have you arrested if you so much as cross the carpet in the hallway outside. Do you understand me?"

"Yes, yes. I just thought that since we were friends and all that I could just come and see you at any time." Jarvis laughed before telling him that they weren't friends at all. "I see. Yes, all right, I'll leave, but you should think about you and Iris."

"That is a done deal. There is no Iris and me. Are we clear on that as well?" Jackson left with the security team, and one of them stayed behind to ask what they were to do about him in the future. "He's not allowed on the property. Not on the grounds, and especially not in my house. If you see him, you have my permission to arrest him and throw away the key."

The man laughed and said that he would gladly do that. "Also, sir, I'm not sure if you're aware of this or not, but someone was in your office late last night. I do believe it was Jackson. Do you want me to run the security tapes to find out? They'll show us how he's getting in the front door, so to speak."

"Yes, I do. I've been told by Burcher that she thought that he was getting much too familiar with this place and I should crack down. The nerve of the man coming here after hours. Look them over, and if you find that he's been in here, I want to know." The man said that he would. As he was going out the door, he was giving information to the other guys concerning Jackson. By the end of the day, hell the hour, Jackson would be blocked from all entrances to the place.

For having such a shitty start to his day, Jarvis thought it was turning out pretty good. So far at least. Pulling out the paperwork to have Iris terminated, along with her arrest, he was just finishing it up when the security team came in the office after a short knock to let him know what they'd found. Iris would be gone with her buddy within the hour as well.

~*~

Hawk looked over the building with an eye for what he

81

had in mind for it. His dad was with him, as was his mom this trip. Jamie was going to meet them here soon. She had gone in to help Lauren with a couple of things. His mom asked him if he was all right.

"Yes, never better. Why do you ask?" She patted him on the cheek and said that she loved him. "And I love you. Very much. What is wrong, Mom?"

"Wrong? Well, I don't even know where to begin." She started crying, and Hawk held her while she did. Looking over her head, he asked Dad what was going on that had upset her. His mom started talking. "Here it is almost summer, and I've not once heard any of you ask me about our annual picnic. I've so much to do to get ready for it, but if you'd rather we didn't have it anymore, I'd like to know now."

"Mom, this is the first time I've heard about an annual picnic. If you remember, until recently, I've not been in the States all that much in the last twenty some years." She looked up at him with a teary face. "Don't cry. Please? It hurts me in ways that I can't explain to you."

Hugging her again, Dad left them alone. Finding something for her to sit on, Hawk waited while she gathered her control. He was way out of his element on this stuff. Women he knew didn't cry — they shot you to fuck when they were upset. But he was pretty sure that his mom wouldn't be like that. At least he hoped not.

"What did you do to your mother?" He looked at Jamie and was relieved that she was there to help him out. But instead, she browbeat him for making his mother cry. "Are you cursing again? You know how she hates that from her boys. Am I going to have to kick your ass again?"

"You just cursed." She glared at him, and Hawk was sure

that he actually felt heat from it. "I didn't do anything to her. She just started crying about some annual picnic that I know nothing about."

"And why is it you've not taken the time to get to know about it? Too busy being all macho and shit? I swear to you, Hawkins, I think you need your head screwed on tighter." He wasn't sure what the hell was happening here, but he knew that he'd done nothing wrong. But he was going to keep that to himself. Instead, he apologized. "For what? You do something else?"

"Why are you all pissy with me?" She slapped him on the arm. "This is getting us nowhere. I haven't any idea about the picnic that's upset her. I don't know why she's crying, and I thought of all people, you'd be on my side."

"I'm forever on your side, when what you do makes sense."

He was ready to join up in the service again and be away from home for the rest of his life. Then he remembered how long that would be. He asked if they could start over. "She wants me to help out with the arrangements. I think. I can vaguely remember something about a bash in the summer, but I don't believe I've ever been here for it. I would like to help all I can."

"I do want you to help me. I would love to have you helping me for a lot of things. You've missed some things over the years." He'd missed them all, and was wishing now that he wasn't going to be here for this one. "You should see it, Hawkins. The entire town comes over, and we have roasted hog and all kinds of side dishes. Everyone brings something to share. And then we have fireworks."

"What would you like for me to do to help?" He was

almost afraid when Jamie put her hands on her hips and glared again. "I'll get the hog and have it readied for your event."

"Yes, why don't you do that, son?"

Jamie was comforting his mom again, and he left. He was a coward, he knew, but he wasn't built to deal with his mom crying. He'd only seen her do that one time before, and that was when he had left for basic training.

It only took him a couple of minutes to get in touch with one of his brothers to find out where to get a hog. It was much more complicated that he'd thought it would be. But by dinner time, not only did he have it set up and ready to roast, but he'd hired someone to come out and dig a pit to roast it on. He was very proud of himself.

His building would have to wait until another time. While his dad, also a coward, helped Mom into their car, Hawk headed to the site where the attempted murder had happened. He knew that Jackson was trying to figure out what had gone wrong with his plans.

Hawkins had gone out to the accident site yesterday morning. And while he could hear what Jackson was saying, mostly to himself, he didn't understand a large part of it. The man was going on and on about the helicopter that he'd hired, as well as the death of those boys. When he got back in his car and then gone to the airport, Hawk had followed him to his home. There he saw Iris. She was crying too, but it didn't bother him this time. He had no vested interest in this woman's feelings. Listening in on them, he'd been hard pressed to not laugh at the two of them together.

"I've been fired." Jackson asked her what she'd done. "Nothing, you moron. Nothing that you didn't tell me to do.

Christ, he was so calm when he was telling me that we were not going to see one another again. Then they came and told me that I'd been terminated for some after hours conduct. What the hell does that mean?"

"You don't think he's the one that found out about the recorder, do you? Holy Christ, did you happen to get rid of the program before you left?" She told him that she'd not been able to do anything but get her purse. And that had been searched thoroughly. "We're in deep shit here, Iris. Deeper than I've been in before."

When he started jabbering again, Hawkins wondered if the man's cheese had slipped off his cracker. He'd heard that in a movie once and was happy that he'd been able to use it. But Jackson was talking about his contacts and what they were going to say about this. Then he looked at Iris.

"You should have told him then that you were going to have his baby. At least that could get you some time there enough to destroy anything on your computer." She said that she'd not ever had sex with him, so she wouldn't be able to describe anything about the man, so that wouldn't work either. Someone would be checking that out. "What were you thinking, then, when I came up with this plan? You should have worked harder in getting him in your bed, Iris."

Hawk did laugh then. For all their planning and crap, they were about the dumbest people he'd ever encountered. Neither one of them had a clue how to cover their tracks—not to mention, they were about as stealthy as a goose chasing someone across the yard.

Jackson started pacing the yard. Hawk couldn't figure out why neither of them seemed inclined to go into the house. But when Iris pulled out her keys and unlocked the door, Jackson followed. Hawk hadn't realized that it was her home and not Jackson's. Going to the deck that they'd been standing on, he listened in on their disjointed conversation.

"I'm going to have to cut corners here. You'll contribute some money towards things or we'll both be homeless." She put her purse on the table and opened the refrigerator. Hawk stood outside the kitchen as she fussed about food and money. Jackson was pacing the open living room now. Hawk watched him over her.

"I really thought this would work out. That I'd be able to put my man in the office and we'd be all set for the rest of our lives. What am I going to do now? He'll surely know that I had something to do with the accident." Iris pointed out, without looking at Jackson, that he hadn't been in an accident. "Yes, he had been. Don't you see? He's playing us. He wants us to ask him about it, and then he'll know that we had something to do with it."

"I had nothing to do with that. I told you when you mentioned the plan that it was too dangerous, that someone might see it, being's how it was in an open area. And you bringing in the chopper to take care of the mess—well, you have no idea how difficult that was for me to get arranged." She turned from the still open refrigerator. "I can't be without a job, Frank. I have obligations and people wanting their money. What am I going to do now?"

"I don't know, honey." Jackson went to Iris and Hawk turned away from their embrace. They were nearly making out. When he heard the gunshot, he turned back to see Jackson dropping Iris to the floor. "You were a burden. I had to do this, honey. I just had to. Don't you see? You were a weak link in my chain of events."

Jackson ran out the front door just as Hawk busted in the back. He might have followed Jackson, but he realized that Iris was still alive. He was sure that she'd not be for long. Her heart rate was slowing even as he tried to save her.

"He shot me." Hawk told her to be quiet. She was losing blood. "There is a safe here. You have to get it open."

"I'm going to call an ambulance for you. Just hold on." Iris coughed once, and blood bubbled from her mouth and nose. "Christ. You have to hang on, Iris. You need to."

"The safe is under the couch. In the floor." She told him the combination. "There are things in there that you need. Hawk, you have to bring him down. Promise me that you will."

"I'm working on it. Iris come on, you have to hold on for me." He pulled out his cell phone and dialed emergency. He told the dispatcher who he was, what his rank was, and the address where he was. She asked him what he needed. "A woman has been shot and she's dying. You have to hurry."

After he told her that they were on their way, he held Iris's hand. But as she grew colder from the loss of blood, her voice was getting lower all the time. Iris told him over and over the combination to the safe and to get the things out of it now.

Going to the couch, he moved it out of the way and pulled up the carpet. It wasn't hidden all that well, but he opened it up and was surprised at how large the vault was. When he reached in and pulled out the medium sized suitcase that was there, he saw that there was nothing else. Taking it to the back door, he put it on the porch back there and called to Jon.

In the five minutes that it took for him to get there, Iris had died. Telling the younger man to take the case to Lauren, he went back to the safe and covered it back up the way it had been. He wasn't worried that Jon wouldn't do it; he was more concerned with whether or not he'd be arrested himself as soon as the police got there.

Hawk was — well, to say that he was armed would have been a gross understatement. He was carrying a gun, and enough other items to take out the entire police force if they were to make a big deal about it. Not that he'd not be able to take care of them without all the weaponry on him, but he didn't want to think about how he'd have to explain it all to them.

In addition to his gun, he had three magazines for it, a knife in his boot, and a wire at the top of his boot that was as thin as a hair, but much stronger. A much longer but thinner knife was on his back, attached with a small covering that held his holster in place. The corded bracelet that he had around his wrist was used to garrote should he need it, as well as tie someone up that he'd not killed, which wasn't often. Hawk had learned the hard way that killing was better than them coming back a second time to take you down.

Calling out to the only person he knew that could get his ass out of this mess, he told Lauren what was going on, what he'd sent to her, and that the police were on their way. He asked her if she could come down there, work her magic, and get him out of this.

I don't know, Hawk. What are you going to give me in exchange for helping you out? I mean, you should owe me something. He growled at her and she laughed. *We're on our way already. Jon brought us the case and I've not opened it, because I thought you'd need us first. By the way, you should know that Jamie is with us. And she's madder than I've ever been when things don't go my way.*

Jamie would be mad, he supposed. He had gotten himself in a pickle, as his dad was fond of saying, and there wasn't any hope for him to come out of this unscathed. He looked down at the dead woman, and wondered if she was going to make this worth his while in the form of the suitcase. He hoped so—he didn't want his Jamie to be mad at him.

When the police arrived first, he was put in cuffs. He had enough blood all over him that it was something that he would have done too. Exercise caution until you figure out who the good guys are. He didn't say anything to them other than he'd heard her scream and had come to find her on the floor, and that a man he knew, Frank Jackson, had been running from the house.

Hawk was glad that he'd reached out to Lauren when he had, because now it looked like he might be going to jail. As soon as she and Jamie got there, he could only sit there and marvel at the way the men were bowing and scraping to her. Not to Lauren this time, but to Jamie.

Christ, Jamie was as bad if not worse than Lauren when she was pissed. But Jamie was so much prettier when she did it. No less caustic, but beautiful all the same. When she grabbed the ear of one of the officers, he thought for sure she was going to rip it off. But she was telling him to uncuff her husband or there would be hell to pay. They were removed immediately.

CHAPTER 7

Jamie wasn't in the best of humor. It seemed as if she was pissed off all the time lately. As she paced the big porch, where she'd come to so that she could cool off, she tried hard to pull in her temper. When Hawk joined her, her first instinct was to hit him. And she had an idea where that was coming from, but she didn't know how to broach the subject with him.

"You all right?" Jamie nodded, but didn't dare open her mouth. She was afraid of what would spew out from her lips. "You want to talk about it? Or are you happier just ripping the heads off the people who are only supposed to serve and protect?"

"I found your books, your journals that you wrote in." He didn't say anything, but she could tell that he was upset about it. "I wasn't searching for them. In fact, I didn't know about them. But when I was looking for one of your shirts to wear, some of them fell on my head when I was reaching for the one on the shelf."

Hawk stared off in the distance and didn't speak to her. Her heart was ripped up by what she'd read in those books.

And the worse part was, where she'd read about her. Not her in particular, but a mate. He was adamant about not having one, and his reasoning was there too. He thought that he was a broken man. And he had wanted to have his head removed before anyone could come along that wanted to be a part of his life.

Jamie wanted to go to him, to hug him and tell him it was all right. And the longer he sat there, the more she needed to touch him. Stepping forward, she reached for him, but he stood and backed away from her. Jamie felt her heart explode in pain.

"You shouldn't have read them. I'm assuming that you read them all." Jamie nodded at him, not sure that she could speak after having her heart broken like it was. "They're *my* feelings, Jamie. You had no right to go through those. They were mine."

"I want to help you. I need to." He shook his head and backed more away from her. Not just physically this time, but she could feel the emotional side of him pulling back as well. "Hawkins, I had no idea that you were going through all that. Why didn't you tell me?"

"I guess I won't have to now, will I? You've gone through all of them, so you know what sort of person I am, what I've done. Did it give you nightmares? It does me, every time I close my eyes. When I have a few minutes to call my own, I see them all there, lined up in a neat row with their eyes open." He moved to the stairs that led out into the yard. "You should leave now. Or I will. You can stay here. I'm not coming back."

Jamie sat there for a long time after he disappeared into the woods. He'd been his cat when he'd jumped off the last step to leave her, and it was the first time that she'd ever seen him as one. She thought about what he'd written in one of the books, the part that he was speaking of before leaving her.

He'd been on a mission to take out a house that was a known home of one of the men that they'd been looking for. Hawk had watched the place for days. Kept track of all the people that came and went from the house. And on the tenth night, ten days without food and only sips of water, he made his way into the house to take the man out.

As soon as he entered, he'd written in the journal, he knew that there were bodies in the place. The smell was almost more than he could take. But he moved through each room, looking for the man that had been on their list for a long time, his gun at the ready.

The man was in the last bedroom down the long hall. Hawk didn't hesitate, but shot him once in the head. The man was dead before he could even lift his own gun to fire back at him. Hawk didn't put his weapon away until he was sure that the building was cleared of living people. Once he did that, he called in the rest.

Hawk had been the one that had been called on when there were lives to be taken. He had claimed in his journals that he was cold, a heartless bastard that gave little to no thought to the people that he shot. Nor did he care that they might have children waiting for them to come home. Hawk had labeled himself as a murderer, and Jamie was sure that he believed that too.

Going into the house, she looked around the bedroom that they had shared. There was nothing here that belonged to her. The man that she'd fallen in love with had taken the only part of the home that she'd wanted. His heart was closed up around himself, and she wasn't going to be able to breach it.

The front door was right in front of her. She only had to turn the handle and she'd be gone from him. Crying, she reached for it and turned the knob. Each step she took seemed as if she was losing more and more of herself.

Jamie walked to town. There wasn't anyone that she could call on to help her. All the people she knew, they were friends or family of Hawkins. Walking blindly, the tears hurting her badly, she thought of what he'd done after he'd been able to clear the house.

The bodies, twenty-three of them, had been brought out of the house by Hawkins and the rest of Lauren's men and lined up. Some of them had been dead longer than the others, but it mattered little. The smell was too much, and several of the people that came to help had gone to the woods to throw up.

Hawk said that he didn't speak to anyone for several days, not even his boss, Lauren, when she'd called out to him. It wasn't that he was sorry for what he'd done, but he did need to think of what he'd seen. Death, it seemed, followed him around a great deal. When he returned to his unit, he didn't say a word about why he'd left, nor did he mention the assignment again.

Jamie had even read where he'd had the encounter with Mackenzie. How he'd ordered her to repair his dead friend before he was sent home. Even though his friend had lost a leg and the majority of the other, as well as his left hand and most of his face, he'd ordered her to work on him. He was pissed at her, blamed her for the way his mom had found her little boy — she had been the one that dressed the dead before they were sent home. And Hawkins blamed Mackenzie for that too.

Then under that it told how he'd made a mistake, that he'd done something unthinkable to a woman that was trying her best to save the men who had a chance to walk out of the place. He'd been cruel to her, caustic even. And when he'd left her the second time, he'd threatened her with nightmares by giving her the picture that he'd taken of his friend's mom leaning over the box that her son had arrived in.

He told how it had haunted him, his treatment of the woman. Mackenzie wasn't his brother's mate then — he had no idea at the time that Jamie would be his either. But Mackenzie had left the service that next day and he'd lost track of her. Lauren had helped her along with the discharge, because she knew that Mackenzie had been responsible for Hawk being put in irons when he'd hit her.

Some of the other entries were disjointed. There was a long rant about the former President Joe Irwin and his buddy, Garth Wilson. He talked about taking them out someplace and making them suffer. To suffer in ways that no one would ever find their bodies again. He described, in great detail, what he'd have done to them given the chance. But he hadn't.

There were entries about his family, his mom and dad mostly. About his brothers finding their mates and how he didn't envy them at all. Having a mate, in his words, was akin to being locked away in a prison cell, and he thought he might prefer that over having someone around all the time.

When she got to the town's limit she moved to the hotel, only to remember at the last minute that she had no money of her own. But she did have his credit cards. Making a turn on the street corner, she headed to the bank. She would finish this once and for all.

"I'm sorry, miss, but I don't understand what it is you wish me to do." She told him, again, to take the cards. "But Hawk put you on his account and had these made for you. Is there something wrong with them? I assure you that Mr. McCullough has a great deal of money in the account if you're worried about that."

"I'm not worried about his money." She just wanted him to take them so that she could go and mend her broken heart. "Just take the fucking cards and return them to him. Or one of his family members. I don't need them."

Tossing them on his desk, she went out into the street again. It was raining now, a perfect way to end her day, she thought. Walking again, soaked to the skin, Jamie thought about nothing but the pain in her heart and soul. For as surely as he didn't want her around, Jamie wanted to be with him more than ever.

It was dark when she came upon the barn. There weren't any animals in it, not even any kind of straw or hay. There was a ladder that she was tempted to go up and throw herself off of, but that would be stupid. And one thing she wasn't was stupid. Going into one of the cleaner stalls, she sat in the corner with her back to the door that had let her in.

She felt the touch of someone trying to talk to her. Jamie had just learned how to block them out, not let them breach her mind. Rolling to her side, she put out her hand and started a small fire, just enough to keep her warm while she rested.

When she startled awake, she found Jon sharing the stall with her. He looked as if he'd been there all the time she'd been resting, and he put out a backpack, which she refused.

"What are you doing here? I'm sure that you have things that need your attention." He took the backpack and opened it. He began pulling out containers of what looked like sandwiches, crackers, and cheese. Then he handed her a bottle of water. "I'm not hungry. Please go away."

"No one knows that I'm here." She felt tears, wasted tears, fill her eyes. "Hawkins is looking for you."

"I'm sure that he wishes to finish killing me off, at least my heart. Go away, Jon. I don't want to have to hurt you." He just smiled at her. She knew that if it came to it, he'd be the winner every time. "I haven't taken anything of his, nor will I repeat anything that I read. You can tell him that if you wish. I don't care."

Jon didn't say anything about what she'd said. Jamie was sure that they all knew what she'd done, and they were upset with her too. When he leaned back against the wall, she sat up more and put the bottle of water on the straw covered floor between them.

"You're going to have a child; did you know that?" Jamie looked at him sharply. "You're carrying Hawkins's child. I won't tell him that either. But I thought that you should know."

"You're only telling me that so I'll eat. I told you, I'm not the least bit hungry." He put his hand on hers and she felt the child there. He was so small that it took her a moment to see what Jon was showing her. Pulling her hand away, she cried harder, but told him it didn't matter.

"Doesn't it? I'm sure that it would to Hawkins if he knew." Jamie touched his hand this time and gave him the entire conversation that she'd had with Hawkins before he left her. "He was angry when he said those things. The child *will* make a difference."

"I'm sure that it would. He's a McCullough, after all. And

97

he'd think, or be made to think, it was the right thing to do and take me in, never letting me be with him, but just take me in so that I'd have his child." She snorted at Jon. "Then what will he do? Toss me out again? Thanks, but no thanks. I'd rather raise my son on my own than be subjected to loving someone so much and be treated like less than a person."

Jon nodded. She asked him if he was waiting on one of them to show up. "No. I told you no one knew I was here, and I didn't tell them where you are. And I won't, either, if you ask me not to. But I will keep an eye on you. Bring you food too, since you're stubborn."

"He hurt me. I know that it was my fault, but he hurt me badly." Jon nodded but said nothing. "I'm going now. Please don't come for me again. You're a sweet young man, but this is between him and me."

"You're very wrong about that, Jamie. When you became a member of this family, your problems became all of theirs, including me." She stood up and told him thanks. "I'll see you tomorrow wherever you stop. I can't let you suffer without food. Although I have to say, I didn't expect you to be such a baby about this."

When he disappeared and a large falcon stood there on the railing around the stall, Jamie turned her back on him and started out of the barn. No matter what she did now, it was better than being unloved by Hawk.

~*~

Hawk didn't speak to any of them, not that he'd be able to insert a word anyway. They were beating him with their words, which he'd come to realize was more painful than a hit to the body. Jamie had left him.

No, that wasn't right. He'd kicked her to the curb and

pissed on her. Not really, but he knew that she'd been hurt. For a moment or two when he'd become his cat, he felt her pain. But like a fool, he'd ignored it in favor of being pissed off at her. Now, not only could he not reach her, but he had no idea where she might have gone. Or how she'd gotten there, for that matter.

"Are you listening to me?" He glanced at his dad and shook his head. "What are you going to do about this? Hawkins, she's out there somewhere and all alone. What if someone with meanness in them comes up on her?"

"I think she can handle herself." His dad looked ready to explode. "I can't find her. I can't talk to her. She's blocked me out. What do you want me to do, just go out and start running around shouting out her name? She was pissed when she left here. And I did it. I should have talked to her instead of what I did. I was a bastard."

"I know firsthand how mean you can be when you're pissed off." He didn't need Mackenzie heaping more onto his head, and told her for the millionth time that he was sorry. "Yes, you say that to me, and I believe you mean it. But you still did it, and I'm betting whatever you said to her, you meant it as well. This won't be fixed with an apology or a bunch of flowers or chocolates. You royally fucked up."

He looked at his mom when she simply sat on his couch. Hawk had no idea why he'd called them when he realized that she'd left him. He'd only gone into the house to get his keys and leave her some money when he felt the coldness of the house. Searching everywhere he could think of, there wasn't any trace of her in the house.

Hawk took the phone from Colin when he said it was for him.

"Mr. Hawkins McCullough? This is Danny Platters at the bank. I have your cards here. The missus dropped them off nearly at closing time last night. I've only just found your phone number." Hawk asked him what he meant, she'd dropped off the credit cards. "She came in here, as I said, and told me to give them to you or one of your family when they came in. I told her that I didn't understand. Then she tossed them on my desk and left. I was in a tizzy trying to find a phone number for you. She was most upset when she left here."

"Did she say where she was going?" Danny said that she hadn't, but he hadn't had a chance to ask her either. "She's left me, I'm afraid, and I'm to blame. I need to find her."

"Well, I don't know what to say about that, I really don't. But my wife left me the one time. It was the only time I was ever upset with her about something. She wasn't to blame either. I had taken my mood out on her, you see. She didn't care for that at all." Hawkins asked him how he'd gotten her back. "Sadly, I wasn't able to. My Caroline was killed. Hit by a car that was going much too fast for her to have gotten out of the way. I tell myself every minute of the day that she didn't step in front of that car, but my heart knows better."

He hung up—Danny sobbed a little, then just closed the connection. Hawk sat there for several minutes, holding onto the handle of the phone, and thought about how he'd feel if anything happened to Jamie. He was a fool, a bastard. And he'd hurt her, hurt the only woman that had gotten through his pain and made him a better man. A happy man. Hawkins stood up and then shifted into his cat. First things first, he had to get her scent. Then he'd find her.

"It won't work." He looked over at Jon, who was sitting

at the table where he'd been. He wasn't sure how long he'd been there, but the ice cream in Hawk's bowl was nearly gone and melted a little more than just being put in the bowl. "You won't be able to get her scent, because unlike you and I, she has none."

Everyone has a scent. I know what she smells like. Hawkins thought about what Jon had said before shifting back to himself and sitting at the table again. He thought about her scent and realized that was what he'd been smelling—nothing, except whatever was around her. "She doesn't smell like anything. I need to find her."

"I'm sure that you do. She's a great person. A nice woman. I think that being with you is just what she needed." Jon looked at him. "Then you fucked that up, didn't you?"

Nodding, he didn't even say anything about the boy cursing. When he got up and rinsed out his bowl in the sink, Hawkins waited for him to continue. But Jon started out of the room and Hawkins called him back.

"You've talked to her, haven't you? You and her, you have a connection because of what the two of you are." Jon told him that when they gave him the drugs they gave them to her first. He got a bit of her from the lab. They would bring the drugs directly to him after she was injected, and her blood would still be on the used needle. He'd been able to find her from the very beginning.

"I tasted it once. They had turned their back on me and I touched her blood to my finger. I could feel her, feel her power. And every time they came to my cell to inject me, I would taste her blood again. She grew more powerful daily but kept it quiet so as no one would lock her up as they had me." Jon sat down as he continued. "The connection we have,

I can find her. And tell when she's ill or other things."

"Where is she?" He didn't think Jon would tell him but was still disappointed when he shook his head. "I need to find her. To tell her that I'm sorry and that I love her."

"As the others said, you will not be able to just tell her that. You have hurt her more than this one time. You have shoved her away too many times to have her think you won't continue to do so." He'd broken her trust in him. Hawkins had no idea how he was going to fix this. "I would say, and this would just be me, but I'd leave her be if you're never going to give her what she needs most from you."

"I can't leave her alone. She's all I wanted in the world." Jon snapped his fingers and one of his journals appeared in front of him. When the pages began to flip, he waited to read what she'd read. When it stopped moving, he looked at the stark words he'd written there when he'd been all alone. Jon told him to read it. "'I would rather kill myself than have a mate. And I will kill the babe too should I find out that she carries my child.'"

"Harsh words, don't you think? Yet she tried to talk to you about it. Even going so far as to tell you that she wanted to help."

Hawkins sat there after Jon left him. If he said more to him, then he'd not heard it. All he could think about was the words that he'd written there, words that wounded someone.

His family had left him at some point while he'd been in the kitchen. Hawkins went up to their bedroom and laid down on the bed. The words there, they were pounding in his head hard enough that he could actually feel it. Closing his eyes, he reached out for her again.

The wall that she had erected was solid. And even though

he was powerful, much more so than his family, he couldn't break through it. It wasn't like him to feel sorry for himself, but he did so now. Lying on the bed that had no scent because someone had decided that she didn't need it.

Getting up, knowing that lying there wasn't going to get him answers, he went to his office and used the web to find out where she might be staying, hoping against hope that she had elected to stay somewhere safe rather than out in the open, where anyone could come upon her. Nothing. She had either changed her name around so that he'd not find her, or she had done what he feared most and was out where she was exposed to anyone and everyone.

Using the Internet again, he called in favors that he had, begging for help to find her. And to tell him where she was. Everyone that he knew was willing to help him even after he told them what he'd done.

It was almost dawn when he finally gave up his search for the night and laid on the sofa in his office rather than go to the lonely bed in their room. But all he did was toss and turn, his body feeling more beat up than before he'd laid down. Getting up, he made his way to the kitchen to get something to drink.

Pouring himself a large glass of tea, he was drinking it down when he turned around. The glass flew out of his hand and hit him in the head, then he was punched in the face. The abuse didn't stop there. Every time he moved, tried to defend himself, he was hit again. His mouth was bleeding, as was his head, when he finally curled into a ball and let her beat him as much as she wanted. When she paused, he looked up at her and told her he loved her. It was the last thing he remembered before he was banged in the head again.

CHAPTER 8

Jamie just barely got him in the chair and tied up before she had to take a break. Christ, he was heavy and big. But she was going to talk, and he was fucking going to listen to her. Or else. She had no idea what the or else was going to be, but she'd cross that bridge when it came up.

Checking the rope that she'd used, it had been his bracelet that she noticed she'd taken apart to tie him up with. And the furnace tape over his mouth made her think she was going to win in this round. Maybe. With him, it was difficult to know.

Sitting in the only other chair that wasn't broken when she'd come at him with her fists, she looked at her bruised and battered knuckles. She might have gone a little overboard when she'd arrived. But to see him standing there looking like he had not a care in the world had pissed her off again. And she figured the only way to get his attention was to knock him into submission.

When he lifted his head and stared at her, she nearly went to him to tell him she was sorry. His left eye was swollen shut — his lips were bleeding. Even his ear had a bit of blood

105

on it. But she didn't move, and when he said something behind the tape, she slapped him hard in the face.

"You deserve that and more. To think that I thought that I loved you. You're a moron of the highest degree, did you know that? You told me to leave you. Told me as if we'd not shared a bed, not had this mind-blowing sex, and you told me that you didn't want me around. How the fuck could you do that?" Jamie started crying and wiped at the tears with a furious wipe. "I should make you sit here for hours for the way you made me feel. And for what? Because you had written something down that I read. Well, how the hell else am I supposed to know what's wrong with you if I don't read about it? You certainly haven't been that forthcoming. And these people that you killed, did they deserve it? Or did you go out and murder random people willy nilly like the idiot I know that you are?"

He mumbled something and she ripped the tape off without any thought to how much it would hurt him. Tears were in his eyes, the sting of the tape evident on his mouth. He stretched his mouth and looked at her.

"I'm sorry." She tried to put the tape back on his mouth, but he was good at dodging her attempts. "I'm very sorry that I did that to you. I'm a fool."

"If you're looking for me to tell you that you're not, then you're fucking stupider than I thought you were. And let me tell you, that's not a fair assessment of you. You are a fucking asshole, and a stupid man too." She sat down on the floor in front of him, her anger getting the better of her. "You do know that I can kill you, don't you? I mean, I'd only have to heat myself up, and poof, you'd be out of my hair and not insulting me again. You're mean."

"Yes, I am. And all those other names that you called me. I've never been better than since I met you. I haven't had to write in the books since you came into my life. I should have gotten rid of them." He looked like he was considering that and shook his head. "No, your reading them is the best thing that could have happened."

"So you could toss me aside, you mean." She doubled up her fist and drew back, not at all sure if she wanted to hit him again. "I'm not a violent person, but you've driven me to be one. Are you happy about that? I'm not. And here you sit without a care in the world, and I was alone."

"I'm sorrier than I could ever tell you about that. And I don't want you to be alone." She snorted at him and got up from the floor. "Are you going to leave me here? It's what I deserve."

She thought about what she'd read about his days in the service, the pain that he had had, and wanted to comfort him. But he didn't need that; he needed a good kick in the ass. And she was going to give it to him.

"You don't get to tell me what you deserve or not. I'll decide." She thought that it sounded lame and pulled out the chair; to sit on the floor was unforgiving. "I've been here for you every step of the way. I've been at your side when you needed it, as well as in your heart. But it meant nothing to you, did it? You didn't care what you cost me, or how I felt when you told me to get out of here."

"I'm so sorry." She told him to shut up. "Jamie, I need you in my life. I want you to come back to me for good."

"I'm not a rug nor a door mat. I will not, not ever, take this shit from you again. If I stay that is. And you will think about whatever spews from your mouth, and about others' feelings, instead of whining all the time about how you've been hurt or your mind is all messed up. You think that you're the only person in the world that has dreams like you do? Or that there are people out there that don't have the support group you have? Some of them even going so far as to kill themselves, because that's all they can think to do." She thought of the one page that he'd written. "You thought about it, just ending your life. And any child that you might create with a mate. Kill a life that hasn't even begun to change whatever sad sack feelings you have for yourself."

"I was in a bad place. You don't understand." He told her again how sorry he was. "You have no idea what sort of horrors I saw and created over there."

"I don't understand, huh? I couldn't possibly have had it worse than you did, could I? You were serving your country because at one time it was something that you wanted to do. To make a difference in the world. Then you found out the reality of it and got your panties in a twist." She laughed, and it hurt her to do so. "I wasn't asked if I wanted to have this shit put in me. I was kidnapped at the age of five to become a testing ground for a kid that I didn't know. I had to steal my every meal. Sleep on the cold concrete, praying that I could make it another day, to be safe from anything that they might put in me. But you had it so much worse, didn't you? Poor little Hawkins wasn't happy with the way his pampered life turned out. Well, boo fucking hoo for you."

"I didn't mean that you had it better than me. I only meant to tell you how messed up I was."

She just stared at him. And when he said nothing more, she let her heat go and stood there in front of him. "Yes, I can see where you might think that I wasn't as messed up as you were. What with you being a whole person and me a monster." He begged her to let him go when she put the flame out that surrounded her body. "I don't think so. I came here with the hopes of making you see reason. To show you what you might miss if I was really to leave you. But there isn't any hope for us. Not anymore."

She turned toward the door and stood there in front of it before leaving him. Jamie wouldn't return. Not to him or anyone else.

Jamie did the only thing that she could think to do, and reached out for Lauren and told her what she'd done to Hawkins. When she explained to her that he was tied up in the chair, she told her to come and get him. Lauren asked her where she was going. Not answering her, she left him there, screaming for her to return for them.

She didn't get far before she was knocked down from behind. The large cat, a jaguar, laid on his belly and stared at her. When she pulled out her gun and aimed it at him, he whimpered again.

"Please don't shoot him." She didn't take her eyes off Hawkins as a cat when Lauren spoke to her from her right. "I was coming anyway after you called me, but he asked me to come here and repeat what his sorry ass is saying." The cat snarled at Lauren and waved his large paw. When he stood up with the hair on his back standing too, Lauren laughed. Like she really found humor in what was going on. "Sit the fuck down before I put you down. You've deserved this from her since the moment you set eyes on her. And you called me to help you, so you'll do it my way, or she'll walk. And I wouldn't blame her." Lauren told him to go ahead and say what he wanted. "Just so we're clear, I'm not going to help you beyond this. You majorly fucked up, and you have no one to blame but yourself." Lauren sat in the grass and nodded at her to begin.

"I have nothing left to say to him. I've said what I wanted to, and I was leaving." Lauren laughed. "What do you find so funny?"

"You beat the shit out of him, he said. Then while he was out at some point, you put him in a chair and tied him to it. Clever that, but you do realize that at any point he could have gotten away, right? I mean, he's a bit stronger than he lets people think he is." Jamie looked at Hawk and asked him if that was true. "He said that it's true, but he wanted to talk to you, and sitting there taking what he deserved was the way that he'd get to say his piece."

"I've heard enough of his pieces. He hurt me." She looked at Lauren. "I'm leaving here, and I'd like for you to make him leave me alone."

"Honey, that's not going to happen, I'm afraid. I can no more make him do anything than I could you. And I'm reasonably sure that if I told you to give him another chance, you'd tell me to fuck off. Right?" Jamie nodded at her. "Yeah, thought so. As I said, it's no less than he deserves, but, and this is just me talking, I think you've made your point with him."

"I don't need for him to tell me he's sorry again. I needed him to love me, like I meant something more to him than a quick fuck. Well, it was never quick with him." She looked at Lauren, completely embarrassed. "I'm sorry."

"No worries." She stood up and so did Lauren. "It's time the two of you had a long conversation, and this time, no beating him up. I'm glad that you did though. Sometimes it takes that to get their full attention. And I'm positive you have his."

"I'm not going to stay here with him. He's already said that he doesn't want me." She felt herself falling back, but strong, warm arms were around her. Jamie could hear Lauren laughing and wanted to hit her a couple of times. But Hawkins had her down on the ground where she wasn't able to move. "Get off me, you lug. I swear, why are you forever knocking me on my ass?"

"You have a pretty ass. I don't think I've ever told you that before. And I do love you." She tried again to get out from under him. "Be still so that I can talk. Think of this as me tying you to the chair."

"I don't want you to talk to me." He kissed her; it was as consuming as it was heady. "You've always been good at sex, Hawkins. We have no trouble in that area."

"No, we don't. And I'd very much like to have no trouble at all, of any kind. I'm a fool, I've said that to you, but I honestly believe it. I have been whiney and a pain in the ass. Had you not pointed that out to me, quite painfully I might add, then there is no telling how long it would have been before someone else did the same thing you did. However, they would have been much harder on me." She said that she'd been very hard on him. "I know, honey. And you want to know the truth? Yours was more from the heart, while they would have done it so that I'd learn a lesson. Yours, I think, hurt me more than any slug I could get from them. And I can't tell you often enough how very sorry I am that you had to resort to violence to get my attention."

"I hurt my hand. Look at it." He took it to his mouth and licked the wounds closed. She told him that it had hurt her in her heart too. "I don't think you can lick that and make it not hurt."

"No, but I can work on that by loving you with all my heart." She didn't feel convinced, and that hurt her as well. "I'm going to bite you if you'll allow it. I want to taste all of you, but biting you will connect us in ways that no one will ever be able to break."

"Why didn't you want to do that before now?" He said that he'd been an idiot. "Yes, you have, about a lot of things. And don't think because you've melted my heart a little that I'm going to let you get by with this again. You're a grown man—you should act like it more."

"You mean like this?" Hawkins rocked his hard cock into her softness and had her moaning. "How about like this? I do love the taste of your breast, the way that it fits into my mouth so that I can bite it fully."

"You're not playing fairly. I'm still mad at you."

Jamie moaned again when he tore her blouse off and lifted her bra up and over her breast. When he suckled just the tip, making her nipple feel like it was on fire, Jamie held him to her as she wished they were both naked. "I need you."

"Yes, I need you as well, love." He slid into her, his body taking over hers on every level. "Give me all that you have, Jamie, and I promise you with all that I am that I'll never trample over your feelings again."

~*~

Hawk felt like a shit. Worse than that, really. He'd made her cry, and she'd hurt herself making a point that he should have gotten long ago. Having her naked and beneath him was the best way to get her to love him again, to trust him. Probably for the first time since they'd come together.

112

He made love to her slowly, fully aware that they were in the yard and completely exposed to everyone and everything. But at this moment, he could care less. Hawk needed her. Needed her more than he'd ever needed anything in the world.

"You're driving me crazy. Do something." He laughed, feeling good about that too. It hadn't been forced in a long time, but today, with her, it felt lighter and more him. "You remember what I did to you in the house? Well, I'm going to do so much worse to you when I get you inside."

"You are a violent little thing, aren't you? Who taught you to fight dirty like this? It wasn't me." He took her small fist into his larger hand and kissed it before showing her how to make a fist that wouldn't break her fingers. "This is how you hit someone. Or you can use a chair leg. That might have put me out longer though."

"I'll remember that the next time you need your diaper changed." He kissed her again, thinking that if he had her like this all the time, she'd never want to leave him. But as she had said, they were good at sex—it was the rest that he'd been a failure at, and he told her that. "You're not a failure, Hawkins. Never that."

"I was with you." She shrugged and he kissed her again, this time showing her how much he loved her. "I'm sorry. I know that you're sick of hearing that, but I can't explain to you how it felt to have you leave me in the kitchen. I was in panic mode, thinking that if you left, I'd never get to hold you, to love you like you deserve. I want children with you, to see you grow large with our children and hold you to feel them."

Hawkins kissed his way down her body, telling her with

113

each taste of her skin what it reminded him of. His hands couldn't be still—he touched, molded, and loved every inch of her. When he finally got to his goal, her beautiful pussy, he kissed her on each hip before he settled between her thighs.

She was wet. Not just that but soaking with her cream. Sliding his tongue through her damp curls, he tasted heaven. Burying his mouth over her, he sucked hard on her clit, then bit down hard enough to have her screaming out his name, bucking him nearly off her when she came.

"Hawkins, I'm so needy. Please, let me have all of you."

He slid his fingers into her as he feasted on her. She was screaming out her releases so many times that he'd lost count. When she was crying while begging him, he moved back up her body the same way that he'd gone down it, kissing and loving every part of her.

"You're so responsive." Jamie told him that she needed him, begged for him to do something to take away the need. "I'm going to fill you. Then I'm going to make sure that you never want to leave me again."

"Please, hurry. Right now I'd take about any punishment just to come hard." Hawkins teased her pussy with his cock. However, his plan to make her beg for more backfired when her heat, her pussy, seemed to suck him into her. "Hawkins, now."

Slamming forward, Hawkins cried out with it. It wasn't painful, but blinding in the way that she seemed to come alive with her release. As he fucked her hard, holding her body to his as he did so, he watched her face. As she was watching him.

"Come with me, Jamie. I want you to tighten around me. Come so hard that when I bite your lovely neck, it only makes your climax better, stronger. Come now, baby."

He nearly missed the opportunity to come with her, the sight of her tight in her release so beautiful it defied words. Leaning into her neck, feeling his cock fill just for her, he bit down at the exact moment that she screamed that she was coming again. Hawkins did as well, coming hard enough that his eyes rolled to the back of his head. He saw stars while he was there, and sparkles when he came.

She clawed at his back, and he could feel the blood as it pooled at his spine. When she came the third time in as many minutes, he came again as well, feeling as if this climax had sucked him dry and put him away damaged. Hawkins dropped over her.

Neither of them said anything for long quiet moments. He rolled to his back, taking her wilted body with his. Still no words were spoken. They both seemed to be lost, or too exhausted to move, much less talk. At least he was.

"I love you, Jamie. Will you marry me?" She raised her head and looked at him. He could see the confusion on her face. "I want you to be my wife, to marry me for richer or poorer, and beat me when I need it."

"Oh, you can bet on that, buster." She laid her head back down on his chest without answering him. "Were you serious about wanting children? I mean, sooner rather than later?"

"I would love a child now, but it's your body and your decision on that." She said that had been taken from her at some point. "You mean the ability to have children?"

"No, making the decision to have a child. It seems that we've already done that." He was too relaxed to try and figure out what she was saying. Having her here with him was the greatest—

Hawkins lifted her off his chest and looked at her. The smile on her face was just as telling as her words had been.

"You're pregnant? Are you sure? Well of course you are. Women, they know this sort of thing. You're going to be a great mom to our kids." Hawkins could hardly contain his excitement as he thought of her heavy with his baby. "This is the nicest gift you could have given me. You're the—" He lifted her up again, more gently this time. "I'm going to be a father. Me. I'm going to be a father because you are a mom."

"That's usually the way that it works out for people that have sex all the time." He nodded and stood up, pulling her up off the ground too. "Are we done talking about this?"

"No. I just want to get you in where it's warmer." She looked at the sky and back at him. "Okay, cooler then. But don't trip on anything. Ah, the hell with it."

Hawkins scooped her up in his arms and told her to dress. When they were both suitably clothed, he took her back to the house and through the kitchen, where the table and all the chairs were broken. He thought of the look on their cook's face, Miss Bean, when she saw this.

"You'll take a nap every day." She laughed. "I'm serious. Having a baby is hard work, and I want you in good health when you have him or her. Which is it?"

"A baby." He nodded, as if that answered his question, as he sat down on the couch with her in his lap. "Hawkins, I'm sure I'm not going to go into labor for a few months yet."

"Yes, but I want to be sure that you're not overdoing it. We'll hire a nurse to come in and take care of you. She'll have one of the rooms on the bottom floor so you can yell for her when you need something. Of course I'll be here, but I'm always in my own—" Hawkins kissed her hand when she put it over his mouth. "I'm going overboard, I guess."

"You think so? I will not take a nap everyday unless I feel like I need it. And you will most certainly not hire a full-time nurse. I'll brain you if you even suggest it again." Hawkins nodded as he kissed her hand, her fingers. Then, lifting her feet, he began to massage them. "That feels wonderful, but you're not off the hook yet. I want you to design our baby's nursery."

"What?" He felt his face heat up when he remembered some of the other things that had been with his journals. "That was just for fun. While I was in a funk, which was often, I'd try to think of good things that I could do. And of course, I wrote them down so that if I ever read them again, I could tell myself that I had some good left in me. I think it was some project we had to do about filling space wisely, and the memory stuck with me."

"I love it. And the way that you built everything out of wood is so impressive that I'd like to put it in the baby's room. As a memento of how his dad was a good architect when he was younger." He told her that he'd thought of that as a career when he'd been about seventeen. Then he'd met up with Lauren. "You were a good soldier, but you're going to be a better father."

"I will too. I mean, how can I go wrong, right? I have you in one corner keeping me in line, and my mom and dad in the other one, begging for me to let them hold our child." Hawkins kissed her again—it was quick but heated. "Have you been to the doctor? I mean, is that how you know?"

"Jon told me. While I was hiding out from you." Hawkins said that it must be true then. "He's a good kid, I'm sure you know that. He told me that he'd not tell anyone where I was, but he thought I was making a mistake by not telling you about the baby."

"You weren't going to tell me?" She put her head on his chest and he held her. He thought about it, and knew that he might not have told him either, not the way he'd been to her. "I can understand that. I was a bastard, and what you read, that couldn't have given you any confidence that I'd be there for you. I'm so glad that you came back to me, Jamie. I love you very much."

"I've never stopped loving you, Hawkins. I was pissed at you, but I still love you." He kissed her again as he sat her on the couch and put a blanket on her. "This shit isn't going to be happening, buddy."

She tore the blanket off her lap and Hawkins laughed. It came from his heart this time. He was genuinely happy. And he was no longer afraid.

CHAPTER 9

Marshall Pennington looked at the paperwork in front of him again. There could be no mistakes this time. If she really was his daughter, then he was going to demand that someone tell him how this had happened. She was given up for adoption, he'd been told. And nobody, not the staff or anyone else, could tell him who it was or who'd taken her to the orphanage when she'd been an infant.

"You've done all the checking? Background as well as financial?" His attorney, Gordon Gibson, nodded. "And this work you have here, I'm not sure what it means to her. Or for that matter, what it means period."

"That's what I'm trying to understand as well. They're medical records that were traced to belong to this woman. Some of those treatments, they're beyond my knowledge of what they might be used for. And I'm still trying to figure out why the now debunked lab had them on their computer hard drive." Marshall had paid dearly for those to come to him. And it was still costing him trying to figure out what the hell it all meant. "I've got your guys looking into this now. They said that they'd have the breakdown of each of the tests for you in a few days. There are a lot of them, Marshall. It won't be rushed because you're excited to have finally found her."

"You really think it's her? I mean, there have been so many since we found out about her. What makes you so sure this time?" Instead of an answer, Gordon turned the file he had to the last page. There was a photograph of a young woman that could have been the double for his mistress at the time. "Christ. And to think how much I kept her when she was fat with my child and I didn't know it. While I never saw her, I continued to pay her rent, give her cash when she asked for it. And now, twenty-four years later, I find out that there was a child and that she'd given it up."

Becky Simpson, his one-time lover, had died about a year ago now. While he didn't remember much about her, and only vaguely could put her name to the pictures of her, she had remembered him, and kept up with his life. When he'd been contacted by her attorney saying that he'd been left a letter in her will, he nearly blew it off as a prank. But it had been her confession of sorts. Telling him that he had a daughter and what she'd done to it.

"She said that she did it to punish me. Had she told me then what I know now, I might well have taken better care of her. I surely would have raised my child." Gordon nodded again, but didn't speak this time. "When do we get to go and see her? Soon, I'm hoping."

"Not for another week or so. The problem is, we're waiting to figure out if she is the same woman that had been in a diner incident where she may or may not have killed someone." He asked him why they were waiting. "If she did it out of spite or something, that'll give us a better picture of what you might expect when you do meet her. Is she a money grubbing woman that will sell off your estate when you're gone? Is she as flighty as your mother? You know as well as I do that the doctor said that it was a faulty gene, and could show up again."

"It doesn't matter to me if she's one sandwich short of a picnic basket, Gordon. If she's my child I will take care that she gets all the care that she needs." Gordon told him that it would be better if they waited just a few more days. "All right. I don't like it, but you do have a point there. I've been busy myself. Doing some research on Becky and what her life had been. She should have stayed put. As soon as she left the home I had provided for her, she was arrested for writing bad checks. I just remembered again, her last name was Apollo. I keep forgetting that for some reason."

"I have other things on her that you might want to see as well. When she was living off your dime, I thought for sure she was scamming you. I found out that she took in others to help with the rent, believe it or not. However, when it came to her having the child, she was able to pay cash for everything, and I figured that was what the cash had gone for."

She hadn't been a greedy lover. It had embarrassed her when Marshall would buy her little things. And when he'd given her a car with the apartment, she refused it. Simply, she told him, that she didn't need it with the bus system practically at her front door.

Then she'd died recently. He was still trying to figure out how that had come to pass. People were unwilling to part with that bit of information. She'd been young when she passed away — he had found out that she was only in her late forties. Marshall was now sixty-seven, and his time was running out.

121

When Gordon left him to take care of a few other things, he pulled out the picture and looked at it. It was uncanny how much she looked like Becky. The hair was as red as it had been on her mother, and the sprinkle of freckles across her nose was the same. It had been what had attracted him to her in the first place. The red hair and the freckles. Since her, there had never been another woman that has sparked his interest like she had.

Not to say that he didn't date when he'd been a little younger. He could have any woman he wanted. Not because of his looks—he was an average man, he guessed—but his wealth. Marshall had inherited his parents' estates and had made good on his promise to make more. It hadn't occurred to him until almost too late that at some point money meant nothing if you had too much of it. So, he began his crusade to spread his wealth around a bit.

He was responsible for the downtown rejuvenation. Also, the new businesses that had popped up when it started to bring more people to the downtown. Where there had been displaced people, most of them homeless, was now a beautiful facility for them to go to, at no cost to them, so that they could shower, use a computer should they want. He'd recently added an education room for those who were ready to finish school. He loved that idea more than any other.

There were many more charitable things that he'd started, most of them small, but others that had made a real difference in quality of life for so many people. Staring out the window of his fifty-third story office building, he looked down at the orphanage that had taken his daughter in. He had a crew now going over the building and making it a landmark. It was already that in his heart.

122

Gordon called him on his personal line when he was just closing up his desk to go home. "You near your computer?" Marshall told him that he'd just shut it down. "I'm sending you some links that I want you to go through. They're concerning the place that your daughter stayed for the first few years of her life. That place was not a place I'd send even my worst of enemies, Marshall. Call me back when you've read them over."

The first article that he clicked on was about the support that the town was no longer giving the place—it had been called Our Lady of Trust when this was written, about twenty years ago. He thought about just skimming through it, but once he started reading bits and pieces of it, he went to the beginning and started again.

The place had been a baby mill. Young charges had been brought there with the parents given false knowledge about what they were actually doing with the children. They estimated that there had been as many as fifty children sold around the world, and no one could speculate on a reason to have done that. He had an idea, but then he'd been around the block a few times himself and knew things that they might not have thought about back then. Some of the children, toddlers and younger, had been used in scientific experiments that had been the home's biggest money maker.

Then a short five years later, the same thing was going on. This time the name of it was William's Home for the Young. He remembered that name now—it has been on the paperwork that had been found on his daughter. The article said that not only were the children sold all over, but again it mentioned that they'd been taken to labs to use. Human waste was what they had called the children that they'd shipped out. The man who owned and ran it said that the city didn't give them enough money to raise someone else's brats, and he'd had to take in more money.

The last article that he started to read had been written only about three years ago. The name then was simply City Orphanage. The city was much stricter this time around, keeping an eye on the bottom line as well as the number of children that went into the place. It all seemed to be on the up and up until the city got wind of the children that were being brought through the back door, so to speak.

City had put out that they would take the children of those that couldn't keep them, with no questions asked and the assurance that they'd not mention where the parents had taken them. This had gone on from nearly the day that they opened. There was no shipping the children out now; they were simply taken to the lab that had been in town only a short while, and never heard from again.

Records had been found. Over two hundred children, most of them older kids that had been scooped up off the street, had been taken to City. Pictures were attached to this article, and Marshall was sickened by the sight of the children that had been tossed aside when they were no longer useable. The pile of bones and half gone bodies made him ill enough to have to run to his bathroom and vomit several times before he felt like he could call Gordon.

As soon as Gordon answered the phone, he told him to halt all work on the building. He was tearing it down. Then he asked about the lab.

"It was raided a few months back. There had been some experiments going on there that I'd rather not talk about." Marshall thanked him, feeling his belly tense up again. "I have it on good authority, Marshall, that this girl that may or may not be your child spent about fifteen or twenty years in the place. Not as a lab tech, but one of the guinea pigs that they used." Marshall closed his eyes and leaned back in his chair as Gordon continued. "There are blood samples of most of the people that were there when it was shut down. I'm having the female ones run now. I know which one her number was, but I'm having them all run so no one is the wiser as to what we're doing."

"Good idea. And when you figure this out, let me know immediately. I don't care if it's in the middle of the night or if I'm in a meeting. I need to know." He told him he'd call him from the lab—he was sitting on them until they were all finished. "Thank you, Gordon. I don't know what I would have done had you not helped me with this search."

"I'd like to find her too, Marshall. I want to see what the child has become." There was a clicking noise, and Gordon told him to hang on. When he came back, it was to tell Marshall that they were getting results. Now all he had to do was wait.

Marshall had never been one to be patient about things, especially when it was something that he wanted done a week ago. This waiting to find out if they'd been chasing their tail for six months was going to be incomparable to anything else that he'd had to wait on.

~*~

Jamie was bored. There wasn't much for her to do with the house. It was beautiful just the way it was. She knew nothing of roses nor the herbs that were in abundance in the garden that was outside of the offices. And if someone would have asked her about the trees and if they needed anything, she would have told them that they were green.

125

The phone was ringing when she made her way to the kitchen. She and Hawkins had decided to wait until today to tell his parents about the baby. Then they'd tell the rest of them, after the doctor confirmed it. They were sure—Jon wouldn't lie to them—but they were taking no chances in telling his family and having it turn out to be a mistake.

"Miss? The call is for you. It's Miss Reilly."

Taking the phone, she was a little afraid of what she might want from her. Jamie knew that she wasn't like the others. They all had some kind of power, but hers was much bigger, off the charts stronger. She said hello when she heard Reilly laughing.

"Just the woman I need to talk to. What do you think about tea and crumpets?" Jamie told her that she had no opinion either way. "Yeah, me either. I don't care for tea, but cold and crumpets? I don't even know what they have in them. But we've been invited to a tea party with Bea. And when I say that, I'm basically telling you that we're being made to go with her."

"You can tell her no, you know." Reilly repeated what she'd said to someone else and the laughter was louder. "What's the joke? I'd like a good laugh about now."

"I'm not like you, or Lauren. I'm not a wimp either, but telling Bea no isn't going to work. Have you told her yet that you don't want to do something or go someplace with her? I'm betting not. You're still breathing." This time Jamie laughed. "You're a great deal like Lauren and are one of those women that takes no shit and kills whatever disagrees with you. Not really, but you two are scary strong."

"I'm opinionated. That's what Hawkins said anyway." Reilly told her that was good and asked if he was still breathing. "For now he is. Who knows about that when he gets home."

She was enjoying the banter that was going on, and relaxed as the call went on. Reilly told her about the tea and how Miss Buttermilk was bringing her daughters to this thing, and Bea wanted to show her girls off.

"There is a love hate relationship between Bea and this Buttermilk person, if you know what I mean." Jamie didn't, but Reilly continued with the reasons they were required to go. "From what I've gathered, Miss Buttermilk—who has a name that is sour milk?—anyway, her daughters look as if they've fell out of the ugly tree and hit every branch on the way down. I didn't say that, but that's the consensus around town. So you're to dress up. We're all wearing sundresses in different colors, and some sexy shoes. I don't have any of those, and I'm sure that Lauren won't even consider it, but that's what we're to do. You game?"

"Sure, I guess so. I mean, I'm not doing anything here but missing Hawkins." He'd gone to help his brothers and dad out. They were trying to get a house done before the vet who was going to live there came home. The house was being outfitted for someone in a wheelchair. "But I don't know about heels either. I'm not much of a girly girl, so there is that."

"Don't worry about it. The rest of us will cover for you if you're asked which tea you enjoyed the most with your crumpets. Who the hell cares is what my opinion is. But for Bea, we'll do this." Jamie asked her how she was going to get there, she didn't drive, and even if she did, she didn't have a car. "I'll have to get on Hawk about that. What are you to do if you can't meet us at the mall at Christmas time? Big deal, Christmas, by the way. Well, all the holidays are. I'll see you in about twenty minutes."

The phone went dead, and she wasn't sure what to do. Jamie had twenty minutes to get sexy and nice looking for a tea? What the fuck was she going to do? Wing it, she thought, and headed to the bedroom to try on different outfits to see which one looked good on her.

Nearly all the twenty minutes was spent on finding a dress. And when she ran out of time, she wore the one she'd thought up first. It looked like she'd just stepped off a fucking cake, but it was bright and cheery, and she compromised with lace up sandals instead of heels. Going down the stairs when she heard the doorbell ring, Jamie was glad that she'd gone with the bright one. She's fit right in with the others.

"Wow, you look fantastic. I love those colors on you." Reese asked her to turn around and whistled loudly. "We're going to knock this out of the ballpark, I think. Bea will be proud of us, and we'll get brownie points. I'm saving mine for when I really screw up."

Reese was explaining to her the points that they were able to earn. Having a baby or bringing one into the family earned the most.

"Since Lauren had four right off the bat, she's been able to curse around Bea and she doesn't say anything. Also, if you have a talent—like mine is baking, and I bring something to every affair. All of us have something that we're really good at. I'm sure you have one too."

"No, I don't cook. I can't paint or draw. I'm pretty much a failure when it comes to plants, and don't get me started on the computer. It buggers up every time I'm near it." She was in the limo now and looked around at the rest of them. "We do clean up nicely, don't we? But back to my talent, I don't have one."

"Sure you do. Your talent is more valuable than anything we could do. You gave her back Hawkins. And trust me when I tell you, even a baby couldn't top that one. She was telling me the other day how much she'd missed her boy and was so glad that you two are happy." Lauren laughed. "I didn't mention how you had beaten him to shit then tied him to a chair. I wish I could have seen that. I would have given my left nut to have been there."

"You don't have any nuts." Jamie thought about it a second. "You don't, do you? From what I've heard, you're really good at busting them, but I couldn't tell you about whether or not you have a set of them."

They were still laughing when they pulled up in front of the country club's main building. She was almost afraid to get out of the car, then she saw Bea. The woman was the nicest person she knew, and Jamie would do this for her without a fuss.

When she saw her, Bea hugged her tightly and told her how happy she was about Hawkins. She told her that since he'd been gone, he'd been a different man, not the child she'd raised. Now, Bea told her, he was his same old self again, and perhaps a little happier.

"I really didn't do anything but set down ground rules." That got the women laughing again, and she glared at them before continuing with Bea. "He's a good man and has a great heart. And I love him. That's all it is."

"Whatever it is, I can't thank you enough for it. Rich and I were talking the other day about our family, and how it's growing by leaps and bounds. I don't think that anyone could hold a candle to how I feel." A large woman with four equally overweight women went into the building in front of them. "That's Cora Buttermilk. She and I have a competition. Every year, we try to outdo the other. This year, I'm going to win. My daughters are shining, and that'll be mud in her eye."

This family was a little more violent than she was, Jamie thought. They were also very competitive. Smiling as they were seated at a large table that held them all, she was glad that she'd come here today. And Bea was right, they were going to win this one. Whatever it was.

Tea was served in tiny cups. Bea had brought them all one to use, and gave them prettily stitched hankies. When Lauren started to take hers to her nose, Jamie thought that Bea was going to have a heart attack. It had been a joke of course. Lauren would never blow her nose on anything but toilet paper, she told her.

Tickets were given out to all of them. Then you could buy more if you wished. The tea party, an event that happened every year, raised money for the library to buy books and such. Last year they'd managed to get enough funding from this to not just buy books for the shelves, but had been able to put in two more computers.

Jamie had cash on her. Hawkins had given her a great deal before he'd left this morning. Watching how many extra tickets the other women bought, Jamie purchased two hundred dollars' worth as well. She had no idea what the tickets were for until they started around the tables with small bags to put their tickets in.

"It's called a Chinese auction. I haven't the faintest clue why it is, but they make a good deal of money for the items that are donated, and it's fun to see if you win." Bea was putting her own tickets in each bag that was out. "I never win anything, but I'm happy to be here with you girls."

"While I have you alone, I have something to tell you." Jamie did the same thing with her tickets. "Hawkins and I are going to have a baby."

Bea didn't say anything, so Jamie turned back to look at her. She was shell shocked, and standing there with her tickets in one hand and holding onto the table with the other. Jamie asked her if she was all right.

"Yes. I guess maybe I didn't hear you right." Jamie assured her that she had as she got to the end of the line of bags. "You and my Hawkins, you're really going to have a baby?"

"Yes. We're not telling anyone else until we were able to tell you and Rich. So, as I said, I'm glad —"

The hug was unexpected but welcome. Jamie hadn't ever had a mother figure in her life and welcomed this woman with her entire heart. "I'm assuming that you are happy."

"I am very happy." Another hug and they made their way to the large display in the middle of the room. "Oh my goodness child, you have no idea how happy I am right now. Hawkins is back with us, and you're having his child. There isn't a thing in this world that could make this day any better."

She put the remaining tickets in the grand prize bag. Jamie would love to win this and give the all-expenses-paid cruise to Bea and Rich. They would have so much fun. Laughing as she made her way back to the table, she saw that the tea and crumpets had been replaced with small bowls of fruit. Now this was what she wanted.

CHAPTER 10

Hawkins held up the drywall as his dad shot screws into it. It was fun working with his dad and brothers, and the work was hard enough that he felt his muscles strain a little after not having much to do anymore.

"You think you might want to join us in our company? Won't take much, really, to work you into the crew. You sure have the muscles for it. Do you happen to lift cars when no one is around?" Hawkins laughed with his dad as he continued to talk about the business. "We have about all of you working with us now. Dustin and I did it by ourselves for a long time. But with the extra hands, we can take on more projects like this one. Does my heart good to see this happening here."

"It is a nice thing. Most of the men I worked with didn't have a pot to piss in most of the time. They were sending the money home to someone. Mostly moms." Dad nodded and asked him where his had gone. "Investments. Land. I had Larson turning it into something more for me. I did send some of my first check to Mom and you, if you remember."

"Heck fire, yes, I remember. Durn near had myself a fit

when that check came in. We sure did set you straight on that one, I think." He said they had. Hawk remembered the call he'd gotten. His parents had been really pissed off when he should have been saving the money for a rainy day. "Jamie settling in with all this?"

"You mean the wealth? I've not told her. I'm not keeping it from her, but she never asked and I didn't think to tell her. I'll do that when I get home tonight." There was a lot of things that he'd not told her yet, and his list was getting longer as the day wore on. "Women can sure turn you into thinking that you're a special person, can't they?"

"Yes, but your mom and I, we knew you was special all along. You were a good boy and turned into a better man." His dad took out his blue handkerchief and blew his nose. "I'm sure liking you being a whole man again. I knew you was suffering a bit, but I couldn't do anything about it. Jamie, she gave you back to us, and I've never been so happy in my whole life."

"We're going to have a baby." His dad looked at him, his face in a comical expression. "She and I haven't told anyone yet, we're waiting to go to the doctor first. But—"

His dad pulled him to him for a big bear hug, and Hawkins held him as he sobbed out how proud he was of his boys. Hawkins wondered if there would ever be a time when him and his mom stopped calling them their boys, but he didn't think so. But that was all right too.

"You gonna tell your mom?" Hawkins told Dad that Jamie was going to do it today, that she'd been invited to the tea party and thought that was a good time. "It sure will be. Your momma, she's going to crow like she's in a patch of corn and there ain't no scarecrow around to make her go away."

Hawkins laughed with his dad, and when he hugged him again, Hawkins hugged him back. It had been a long time since he'd welcomed any kind of hugs or words that meant they loved you. He was glad now that he and Jamie had decided to tell them this way.

They worked on the house for another four hours. Hawkins was going to pick him up some dinner on the way home, as Jamie wasn't going to be home until later. The women had decided to have dinner when the tea was over, and Hawkins was glad that she was having such a good time.

"Wanna join us for some pizza?" Hawkins first instinct was to say no to Colin. But he was learning to be with his family, thanks mostly to Jamie. "The women won't be home until late, and we thought it might be fun to have some manly time together. Jon is going to join us too."

"I'd love to."

It was getting easier to say yes. Not all the time, but that was all right too. He was a grown assed man, he'd been told, and his family missed him. Jamie sure had a way of making a man feel like he meant something. And she meant it, too, when she said that she loved him. He loved her as well.

When they were seated at the big table, he looked over the menu. Hawkins couldn't remember the last time he'd eaten in a restaurant that he didn't have to worry about it blowing up, nor that he was going to be poisoned. When he ordered first, Hawkins order a large pizza for himself. When one of the others asked him if he was sharing, he told them to get their own.

And they did. They ordered ten large pizzas in varying flavors, and asked for a few beers. Hawkins declined the beer in favor of tea. He didn't drink at all, and would like to keep it that way.

Since there were no leftovers, which really surprised Hawkins, they were set to go. But Dad started talking about the next job they had and what was going to be required of them to set the house up. They all looked at Hawkins when Dad explained that the house was for a couple, and that the woman, the vet, had lost an arm and her leg due to a landmine.

"I don't know them. I don't think so anyway. Why are you waiting on me to say something?" He started to get up and leave when Duston told him what they wanted. "I can see what I can find out. I mean, losing both would have been a horrific accident, but the service is very good about training someone on a new set of skills to walk and get around."

"I know that she'll need to have some of the rooms outfitted for her using a wheelchair." Hawkins told his dad that she might have a prosthetic leg and arm. "I never would have thought of that. See, I knew having you come on would be good for us. You find out what you can about this couple, and we'll work from there."

He had a few contacts still in the VA hospital overseas. Most of the people there were just waiting to be sent home. A lot of them, like this woman, would be learning how to cope with life now, and with having their family around. It was more difficult, he knew, to acclimate yourself to family life than it would be to the Army. But most of the men and women didn't have the support group that he had when he'd gotten home.

The house was going to be started on, the foundation poured and the bathroom readied, while he found out what he could. His list was getting longer by the minute. At this rate, he'd be working on this well after midnight. Laughing to himself, he figured that it was a fair trade off to be home all the time. And to be needed.

When he heard from Jamie about her tea party, he wanted to go home and be with her. But she told him that they were discussing some kind of event that his mother was throwing. An annual fundraiser for the library. Since it seemed that he'd be out of place, he went home with his dad to watch some television with the rest of them.

Instead of watching what was on the television, he thought about the work he had going on for the president. This was his last job, he'd told him, but Jarvis seemed to slide over him quitting right now.

"There is a great deal that we can accomplish with you. I don't want to tell you that the world is depending on you, but it somewhat is. This one man, Jackson, can bring down my house of carefully laid cards in a single heartbeat. He has been in my offices, and I don't know, in addition to the paperwork that he took, what else he might have found when he was here looking before we were able to figure it out." Hawkins asked him what sort of things he had kept in there. "Passwords for one thing. And since they were still in there when I looked, I haven't any idea if he'd made a copy of it and returned it to the safe."

That was true, and something that was bothering Hawk. He and Lauren had yet to get together on the suitcase. She had looked through it but wanted his opinion on some of the things in it. There was also money, a great deal of it, and passports — seven in total. He wondered if it was a case filled with things Jackson would need to run. And where was he?

The tracker was still on the car, and it was currently still sitting in the front of Iris's home. They'd done a quick search on it but had left it there in the event that he came back for it. Hawkins didn't think that he would. Jackson might be a moron, but he wasn't that stupid.

There were other things, too, that he had to work on. Like this thing with Jamie's father. He'd had a search going for him for the past several days, but there was nothing that he could find. Hawkins trusted that Jon had the right information and that it was correct, but locating the man was becoming harder and harder.

"Are you paying attention?" He looked at his dad and noticed that everyone else had left them there. He asked if they'd gone home. "They have. You were deep in thinking. Anything I can help you with?"

"I don't know, to be honest. There are several things that I can't talk to you about, but I can tell you that Jamie's biological father is looking for her, we think." Dad asked if they thought he was looking or that they thought it was her father. "Both I guess. Jon came to me a few days ago with the information. He didn't tell me where or even his name, but you know as well as I, if there is anyone looking, he'd know it."

"Yes, he's a smart one, my grandson. What do you know so far?" Hawkins told him that they only knew that he might be in Columbus, and that he only just started looking for her. "You think that he's had a change of heart? Or something that you aren't telling me?"

"My opinion or theory, however you want to think of this, is that I don't think he knew about her. I have no idea why, but that's what I'm thinking." Dad nodded and didn't say anything more. "I haven't told her yet, along with a few other things. But this, about her father, is the only thing that I sort of feel guilty about. The rest, I haven't thought of telling her until today."

"Your money for one thing. I talked to Larson, and he said that you've done very well for yourself, and he doesn't think that you'll slow that down much. He didn't tell me an amount, mind you, but he did say that you were far better off financially than the lot of us together."

"I am." He waited for his dad to ask, somehow knowing that he wouldn't. "The government paid me very well when I was in Special Forces. And I didn't buy anything with it other than my house. As I said, I've had Larson playing with my money, and he's done well with it. I'm a billionaire several times over."

~*~

Jamie was just going up the stairs to bed when she heard the car pull into the garage. She ran back down the few that she'd gone up and met him at the front door. He picked her up and swung her around until she was dizzy with it. Laughing, he set her down on the floor again.

"Did you have fun tonight? I'm betting that you were slightly overwhelmed with it all." She laughed and told him that it was a bit much at times. "Mom said that you won a few things. I had no idea that there was anything going on with it other than tea."

"Oh yes. They have this charity thing, I guess, that will buy books for the library. They have people from all over to sponsor it, and they give the donations away in a Chinese auction. I wasn't sure that I should have spent the money, but it was for a good cause." He told her that was one of the things they needed to talk about. "Not yet. I want to show you what we won. And ask you about one of the prizes. I won a lot of silly things, like a shirt with a movie gift card with it.

Free popcorn at the grocery store when I'm in there, as well as the grand prize."

She had him follow her into the living room and showed him the gifts. It really had been fun, and when they pulled her number out of the bag for the grand prize, she'd been as shocked as the rest of them at the table.

"Did you know that your mom has never won anything at this until tonight?" Hawk told her that he hadn't been aware of that because he'd had no idea that this was going on. "Yes, Lauren said that as well. You weren't home much, were you?"

"Not really. I mean, I'd come home for some rest and relaxation — they called it R&R — but I did neither of them while here. I mostly hid from everyone and bemoaned the fact that it was much too noisy for me." She nodded, understanding completely after tonight. All the people stuffed into one large room had been too much for her too. "So, how did Mom do with the competition? I heard Dad say that it used to be funny, but now it was like they were at war."

"You'd think that too if you saw these big women. I think Cora was most upset when your mom started pulling out pictures of all the grandkids. That really set her off. None of her daughters are married yet, so that was a lot of points in your mom's favor today." She sat on the couch with Hawkins and handed him the flyer for the grand prize. "I'd like to give this to your parents. If you don't mind."

"They'd love this. But are you sure you wouldn't like to use it? We could go on a nice honeymoon if we wanted." Jamie watched his face. "Honey, give it to them if you want. It was your gift that you won. I really think they'd love it."

"I know that it was an expensive day out for me, but I

140

did have a great deal of fun." He asked her to wait there a moment, and left her to go into the hall. When he returned, he had a thick file envelope, as well as a small fireproof box. "What on earth is that for? You couldn't get much in there but a few sheets of paper."

He handed it to her with the key. "That box there holds all the deeds to the properties that we own. At the time that I purchased that for Larson to use, it fit everything in it nicely." Jamie pulled out property deed after deed. She asked him if this was real. "Yes. I've been paid well over the years, and I had no one back then to send it to. The one time that I sent home money for my parents, I got a scolding call from them on saving my money. So, I did."

"Hawkins, there must be thirty deeds here. Surely you don't own them all?" He said that he didn't. "I mean, it's a good thing, but really out of my league, I think."

"I don't own them all. We do. I'm having Larson put your name on all the deeds so that you will own them with me. And anything in the future, you'll be owning those as well." She looked at him, knowing that the next question was going to make her nuts. But she asked him how much he was worth. "We are worth, Jamie. What's mine is yours, and whatever you have it's yours as well. Having you is more than enough. And not counting properties nor anything that Larson is working on now, we've enough money to live for a very long time without having to worry about money again. Last I had any figures from my brother, we were worth ten billion."

"Ten million. You meant to say million, not billion. Right? Please tell me that was what you meant." He just shook his head. "Ten billion dollars? Are you fucking serious?"

"As I said, that doesn't include any of the property that we

141

own." Jamie got up to pace the room. This was just too much to handle right now. She'd been worried about what he'd say when she spent two hundred on tickets, and it wouldn't even make a dent in what he had. "Are you all right?"

"I have no idea how I'm supposed to feel right now. I cannot even imagine what ten billion looks like." He reminded her again about the property. "I remember. Trust me, I'm dealing with this one thing at a time, thanks. Is there anything else that I need to know?"

"Yes. We think your biological father is looking for you." She sat down on the floor, and he hurried over to find out if she was all right. "I've known about it for a few days, and there never seemed to be a time when we weren't either running out the door or in the middle of something else. I'm so sorry."

"It's all right. Just tell me, is it my father, are you sure? Or one of the other jackasses trying to find me? They could be pretending to be him to catch me off guard." He said that was a possibility that they've thought of. "Who? You and Lauren?"

"So far as I know, Lauren hasn't any idea that we're looking into this. Another thing about having no good time to do it. Jon came to me and told me about it. He explained that he could feel someone searching for someone that had been an infant turned over to the orphanage where you had been." She asked him how they thought it was her. "The dates are about right that you would have been dropped off, from what we can tell, and since someone is working on the building, the paperwork has been put in the library for people to look at. Did you know that the place had changed hands a couple of times over the years?"

"I sort of knew that. When I was there, it was called Lady

of Trust or something like that." He told her. "Okay, Our Lady of Trust. You have to remember, I was five when I was taken away. I remember the place, but I don't think that I could take you through there and show you where things were."

"I don't know the name of the person, your supposed father, to go and talk to him about this. All I know for sure is that someone is looking." She tried to wrap her mind around all this. Hawkins was a billionaire. She was too, she supposed, but holy shit, that was a great deal of money. Her father was out there someplace. And he was looking for her. "What are you thinking about?"

"Everything and nothing. I was going between the money and my father. When I was a little girl and trying my best to stay out of the notice of the men in the lab, I would dream about the two of them coming for me. You know, to rescue me from all that was being done to me. Then, not too long after I realized that I was a monster, as I thought of myself, I was glad that they'd not looked for me. What do you think they'd say if they were to see me how I am now?" He asked her what she meant. "You know, this person who has these freaky abilities to turn into a human flame with a single thought. I can read minds, and also those of the people that they might have touched. It's a lot for me — I can't imagine what it would be like for a human."

"Yeah, when you put it like that, it would be a little scary. But they'll also see what I do. A determined young woman who is smart and resourceful. A beautiful being that can be a debutante one minute and kick someone's ass the next." She pointed out that might not be a selling point to most people. "It is to me. I don't worry about you getting hurt. In fact, I hope that no one pisses you off so that I won't have to go and bail you out of jail."

Sitting on the couch with him again, she put all the paperwork back where it had been. It still boggled her mind, the amount of money that Hawkins had. When she had it all put away, she laid down on his lap while he played with her hair.

"You going to sleep?" She told him that she was thinking. "Can I give you something else to think about?"

"Is it Jackson?" He said that it was. "I know that he's still out there and will need to be captured, but right now, I don't want to think about him or anything else. Oh, I told your mom. She hugged me about a dozen times today, but she didn't tell anyone else. She said that I was important to her because I gave you back to her. I guess you were more whiney to her than you'd been to me."

Hawkins tickled her until she begged him to stop. While she was on the floor and him still on the couch, Miss Bean cleared her throat and smiled at them both. Hawkins asked her if he could help with something.

"Yes, I do believe you can. I need underlings, sir." He cocked a brow at her. "That's what we call those in the kitchen that work with us. They're not the main cook or in charge, but they are still a very important part of the household."

"What would these underlings do for you? I'm only asking because I have a few people that could use a nice place to work." Miss Bean told him what they'd do for her. "That wouldn't work for these people. They're in wheelchairs permanently. But if you think we need more people working here, then I say you should do it. I would imagine that a house this large is a bit on anyone, young or older." Miss Bean said it was the stairs. She could get up and down them, but it took her a while. And when making the beds up there and doing a quick clean up of the bathroom, the stairs were hard on her. "Then hire people, however many you think, to do the work upstairs. I'll have to run background checks on them, just so you know."

"I wouldn't have it any other way, sir." She started away, but turned back to smile at them both. "This house, it's beautiful, but it could use a few touches here and there. You've not a single picture hanging of your lovely family, nor is there much in the way of color in a great many rooms. If you'd like, missus, I can help you with that."

"I'd love that, Miss Bean." She told her to call her Mildred. "All right, Mildred. When we get the staff squared away, we'll work on making this house beautiful. And could you hire someone that could work in the gardens in the back of the house? They're in dreadful shape."

"Oh yes, the gardens here are in sorry shape. I have someone just in mind for that. My husband, Donald. He so loves to work in the garden around the house. This will be a project for him so that he can stay out from under my feet."

She was still mumbling about men and getting in the way as she walked away. Hawkins looked at Jamie and they both burst out laughing.

"I've no idea what to do with a staff." He said that he didn't either, but she sure looked like she did. "We'll see when they all threaten to quit because I'm a hard ass."

"Nah, you got this. Now, why don't we go up to bed and work on a sister or brother for our baby?" She laughed when he picked her up in his arms. "You are going to enjoy this so much."

She was sure that she would. And so would he if she

had anything to say about it. Jamie was as happy as she'd ever been, thanks to this entire family. She wondered how she had managed before they came into her life. Jamie didn't know, but she had them now, and was going to cherish every moment with them that she could. She'd think about the rest tomorrow.

CHAPTER 11

Frank ate his meal with his head down and his mouth shut. He had been coming into this little dive for the past three days, and was amazed that they stayed in business at all. The food, he thought, wasn't fit to eat, and the coffee was from a pot. Who drank from a machine that had to be as old as the waitress that had served him?

"You want a piece of pie, honey?" He shook his head and finished up his meal by mopping the plate clean with his roll. That was one thing that was good, the bread. He could have made a meal from that alone. "Are you sure? We have some fresh baked cherry and blueberry."

"No, thanks." He'd also been a good deal politer when he spoke to people. He was positive that they were out looking for a well-dressed man that spoke with a weird accent. "Just the check."

He waited on the check while he thought about Iris. Frank was regretting killing her now. She might have been able to put him up for a few days. Now he couldn't go near her place, or his, without a thousand cops surrounding him.

There was a cruiser parked in the front of both houses like they lived there. It was despicable the way that the city was wasting money on him.

Okay, Frank thought, he had killed Iris recently. And he had stolen paperwork from the president too. Also, he'd bugged the Oval Office, something that he was regretting more and more every day when he saw his picture on the news at night. The paper had been plastering it all over the place too. This just wasn't in any way helping him.

After she brought his bill, he shuffled his way to the cash register and thought about all the shit that he'd lost with this deal. He'd been paying off people to help with his venture. Then there was what he'd put out to make himself look good. Also, he'd been giving Iris money for helping him out. Fat lot of good that had done him—she'd lost her job, and his finger on the pulse of things at the White House. There were other expenses as well. The money for the camera, as well as the program to set it up. Another thing that hadn't done him a lick of good.

He paid his check with cash and moved down the street to the hotel that he'd been staying in. As soon as he was in his room and the door was shut and locked behind him, he pulled off the scratchy wig that he'd bought cheap and the scarf that had covered most of his face. It was nine thousand degrees outside, he'd bet, and he was forced to dress like it was ten below so that no one would shout out that he was having dinner beside them. People were just too happy to point out other people's faults, when he was sure they had just as many.

Frank had tried twice now to get past the guards at the front gate of the White House. He'd had such an easy time of it before, and now they were treating him like he was a criminal. Didn't these people know that war time was the best time? It was the biggest money maker there was.

"Fuckers." He hadn't been one to use that sort of word before all this. But he did so love the way that it just seemed to roll off his tongue. He said it several more times as he took off most of his clothing and turned the air conditioner up to full blast. Christ, would it ever cool off?

He'd been plotting and planning for several days now. The way he had it figured was that in about a week, maybe less, they'd forget all about him and the cars in front of his house would be gone. Then he'd go inside and get his stash, make a quick stop at the White House and kill the president, and be on his merry way. It was a good plan, but it lacked any way for him to execute it in a way that didn't get him killed or in prison.

Frank had spent quite a few years behind bars when he'd been younger. Changing his name hadn't been that big of a deal when he'd gotten out, not really. He'd just taken his father's first name and his mother's maiden name. It had been that simple. What had taken the longest was getting himself a portfolio, so to speak, that made Frank Jackson a real person. He'd created an entire persona, by just putting his name in a few of those sites for people to chat about stupid crap and order a few things from some obscure company, to establish himself as Frank Jackson.

He didn't even think about himself any other way but as Frank Jackson. As far as he was concerned, Robert Goodall was as dead as Iris was. Laughing as he leaned over the air conditioning vents to cool off, Frank thought that the men looking for him—because there was no doubt that someone would be chasing their tails about now — would be running into dead ends more times than a blind man would hit a building.

Tomorrow he was going to go by the post office. He'd ordered some money from his overseas account to be sent to him via a cashier's check. He figured that was the safest way for him to get it. Calling in a favor to have another new identity made so that he could go and collect it had been expensive, but well worth the trouble. He'd be able to get himself a gun, a passport, and something to drive away from the White House when he killed Jarvis.

There was so much money riding on the fact that he wanted his man in the office of the president. He had guns lined up to sell to either side that had money. And just recently he'd been able to buy some meals ready to eat — the slang for them was MREs. He had gotten them dirt cheap, and was going to provide the other side with them. Sure, they were expired, but he didn't give a shit if they got sick. This was a money maker for him. And truthfully, that was all it was about. Money.

There was still the trouble of getting to the fucker in the Oval Office, however. Jarvis had been hard to read, and harder still to get him to do what he wanted. Like dating Iris. Then to bed her. Once she was on the upper floors there would have been plenty Frank could have done from there as well. Killing the president had only been a thought — now it was necessary to make things fall into place.

"Stupid cocksucker is still fucking with things that don't concern him. Well, I suppose that they do, but I don't care what he wants or needs." Frank thought about how him killing old Jarvis would concern him, but not for long. "He'll be dead a while before anyone knows who did it."

That was the plan, anyway. He was going to blame it on anyone that he could. Not just blame, he said to himself, not with words, but he was going to put enough evidence around the place that it would look as if one of his aides had done it.

Trying the password again on the computer that he'd snatched up the other day, he was disappointed to find that he had only two more tries before it locked up. He thought that he had it right. The one that Iris had used to get to Jarvis's calendar was proving to be a no go too. Maybe he'd just written it down wrong.

Frank knew that he'd have not changed it. The moron hadn't changed the password on the safe after he'd taken over, so why the hell would they think he'd have any changes made to his calendar? That would have been the first thing Frank would have done, so thieves like him weren't able to get to stuff.

He looked at the password that had once gotten him into the calendar. Taking his time while putting it in, he made sure that the caps lock wasn't on, nor were there any other capital letters that might screw him up. And when it told him that the password was wrong again, he wanted to toss the sucker out the window and be done with it. When the computer dinged at him, he sat back down to work, since he was sure that it had worked this time.

"*Hello, Robert. How's it hanging on you? Low and to the right? Or high and to the left? Either way, you're so fucked right now.*" He asked who this was in the little message box that was blinking. "*Your worst nightmare coming true.*"

He wanted to ignore the blinking light, but he knew that whoever it was they might be wanting to help him with his projects. Of course, they had said he was fucked, but he wasn't worried about that. No one knew him or where he was. It was worth a shot to be able to get to his money and things. Then he read back what the first message was. He'd been called Robert. That was bad.

"*Are you going to help me with my plans? If not then just go away. I'm trying to think for a minute.*" He didn't feel that was giving away too much, so he read it twice more before hitting enter. The name bothered him, but it could have been that they had the wrong person, and he'd just happen to have caught it.

"*You mean the password to the presidential calendar? You're not going to get that. I've changed it and put it on a program that will tell me when someone is fucking with my work. That would be you in case you didn't know already.*" He asked the person if they were lying. "*I don't lie, and just wait a minute or two and I'll have the address where you are.*"

He didn't believe that for a moment. No one could put programs on computers that would trace someone. When the person started typing again, and the little cursor was moving back and forth in the box, he went to get him a cold bottle of water while he waited. He opened the curtain a little and saw that there were a few more cars in the lot than there had been a few days ago. Frank was glad; it would make it so he could blend in more.

Sitting back at the computer, he realized that his screen had darkened. He had no idea what Iris had set this thing on to go dark like that all the time, but he was sick of waking it up all the time. He looked at the little box, and crushed his bottle of water in his hand and all over his boxers when he read what was there.

"Well, Robert Goodall, you're at the Winding Oak Motel out off the interstate. I don't know which room you're in yet, but I will before the cops get there." He grabbed up his computer and his pants and went out the door. He had no idea how long it would take for them to get to him, but he was so out of there.

Frank was going behind the dumpster when he heard the first siren. There were at least a dozen cop cars, the SWAT team, as well as the bomb squad. He didn't have a bomb, but he was sure that he would have blown it up before now if he had. Christ almighty, they were all over the place. He pulled on his pants as he watched the goings on around the hotel.

~*~

"I don't understand." Lauren asked Jamie what she didn't get. "Why did you tell him where he was and that you had the cops coming? I mean, you knew that he'd run, didn't you?"

"Yes, that's what I was hoping for. Because now he doesn't have anything. When they looked over the room, they found his planner as well as his keys. We don't know what they might go to, but it's something. They're making copies as we speak. Also, the planner, from what I've heard, is where he's written down his plans for Jarvis. He's got a one-track mind, the moron." Jamie leaned back in the chair that she'd been sitting in. "Thanks for helping us out with this. We might not have ever found him had you not helped. This mind thing you and Hawkins can do, it's pretty useful on a lot of things."

"I had no idea that I could do that until one afternoon when I was waiting on people at the bar where I worked, and this guy came in that couldn't talk. All I did was touch him and bam, I got a shit ton of more things than I ever wanted." She asked her about the computer thing. "That's very new. I just tried it and it worked. Now that I've had a little more

153

practice at it, I'm getting faster at tracing things and people."

Lauren had been around Jon when he'd been practicing with some of the things that he'd gotten. But it scared her a little to think about the power that Jamie had. She was a human flame, and someone to be terrified of.

"Don't be afraid of me. I don't think I could stand it if you and the rest of them were afraid." Lauren told her that she wasn't afraid, but thought that others would be. "Yes, but to them, I'm just an ordinary person that married a very rich man."

"I heard that." Lauren laughed a little. "If you don't mind me asking, when you were in the house searching for the babies, why didn't you take the bastard out with one of your powers? I mean, you have them—why not use them?"

"I didn't know where the babies were, and I thought that he would tell me before I murdered him. And I would have killed the fucker too. Not really, but that's what I was hoping for. To find them and make sure that they got back with their parents safely. I'd been tossed to the curb—no one else should have to feel like I did." Lauren nodded and watched the body cams of the cops looking for Jackson. "You do know that I can tell them where he is, right?"

"Yes, and I'm pretty sure that each of them knows that he's behind the dumpster. They're under orders not to find him. If they happen to stumble on him, that's fine, we'll go with another plan. But in my experience, people make more mistakes when they're as stupid as this man is. And when they're afraid." Jamie said that she could see that. "In a little while they're going to leave, but one of them is going to stay behind until morning. We don't want him to have a nice place to sleep either."

Lauren watched the cameras that had been attached to each of the vests the men and women wore while working. Some of them were her people, the rest were locals. She had asked for help only to play nicely with the people that she might have to deal with on a daily basis. Lauren knew that she could play nice in the sandbox, but she didn't like to.

"May I ask you something? It's nothing to do with this project of yours, but it's something that I've been thinking about." Lauren turned to give Jamie her full attention. There was something very sad in her voice, and Lauren wanted to help her any way that she could. "I'm going to have a baby. And I'm worried, now that I've thought about it, about whether it will be like me. In fact, that terrifies me a great deal. I would rather it's not. It could be dangerous for a child who might not understand."

She thought about what she was saying. There wasn't really a question there, but Lauren understood what she was asking in a roundabout way. She wanted to tell her that a child would be fine, but who knew with the power that Jamie had?

"Congratulations on the baby. I bet that Hawkins is happy." Jamie's face lit up, and Lauren understood that she'd not talked to him about this. "What if the baby has your powers? I mean seriously. If you're worried about it being unable to handle it all, the way I'm sure that you were at first, the child will have you and Hawkins there to train and teach it. Also, how to be careful with where he or she uses it."

"It's so much, Lauren. You have no idea the extent of magic, or whatever this is that I have. I mean, you have every reason to be afraid of me. I am at times too." Lauren asked her to tell her some of it. "I've figured out how to become a bomb in addition to the flame. And I don't get injured. And that's something else. Do you have a knife?"

Lauren leaned over and took one out of her boot. Giving it to Jamie, she was impressed at the way she handled it. This knife was thin and long, and sharper than a razor. She'd used it a few times to kill someone quietly and quickly. When Jamie sliced it over her hand, deeply, the wound healed almost before it could bleed.

"Holy shit, girl. That would be damned useful out on the field." She looked at Jamie and realized that she'd said something wrong. "I'm sorry. But if this worries you, you'll have to tell me how. Because all I can see is an advantage to saving you from bleeding to the point where you can't defend yourself."

Jamie stared at her for several seconds. And for the first time in longer than she could remember, she felt uncomfortable with it. When she finally smiled at her, Lauren did the same. She was a deep thinker, Lauren knew that about Jamie, and was glad that she'd worked it out.

"I never thought of that before." Lauren said that she was forever thinking of ways to keep her ass covered when there could be shit flying around. "I can see that about you too. Perhaps I need to think more like that. I mean, the only person that I'm sure is looking for me is a guy that says he's my father. But that's it."

"Jon had a lot of lab fuckers searching for him when he first came here. It wasn't until we killed him off in a fiery explosion that we were able to bring him back as his cousin, or something like that." Jamie asked her about the death. "His mother, this fucking cunt, was trying to capture him so that she could use him for evil. No one here wanted that, and we took him out of the picture, along with his mother and another male. But back to this man saying that he's your father. Why wasn't I in on this?"

"I'm sure that you will be." Jamie laughed and told her to stop pouting. "I'm sure that Hawkins wanted to be my hero. You are forever saving this family's ass."

"There is that." Lauren asked her what she knew. "I mean, I can find people better than most. You tell me what you have, and I'll look around. That way if—or *when*— Hawkins comes to me, I'll be one step ahead of him. And I so loving being ahead rather than behind in research."

"I knew that about you as well. I like you, Lauren. I mean, hanging out with you is great, and you don't hold back when you have something to say." Lauren thanked her. "I like the others too, don't get me wrong, but I have nothing in common with them. Not really."

"I don't know about that. You seem to have a knack for making Bea smile." Something occurred to Lauren. "You told her, didn't you? About the baby, the day of the tea party? Hot damn, I'm good—you did."

"I did. Hawkins told his dad the same day while he was working with the others. We wanted them to know first. Then we were going to tell the family later." Jamie glanced away before looking back. "You're not mad about it, are you?"

"Oh, hell no, I'm not mad. I love that you told them first. It seems sort of fitting that you did it that way. Hawkins isn't their baby, but they've missed a great deal of time with him. Even when he was home, which I don't think was that often, he was missing to them." Jamie told her that Rich told her that she'd given them back their son. "You surely did that. He and I, we've spent a great deal of time together over the last ten years or so. I got to know everything there is to know about him. Even off work, we'd hang out together. And I noticed the change in him now that he's home and I see him now. But it was over time. Not an all of a sudden change, but a gradual one that snuck up on me."

"He's excited to be a dad. I am too, about being a mom. Just worried what parts of me the child will get." Lauren smiled. "I mean the parts of me that were put in me, not my personality."

"Yes, well, you and I have about the same sort of personalities, I think. We don't suffer fools well. We're not afraid to let people know how we're feeling, and when someone else has a better idea, we don't run them down with our way or no way. That shit will get you killed almost as fast as a bullet can travel." Lauren watched her laugh. Jamie had a good personality to go with her tendency to be like her. A good balance, she thought. "I'll be looking into this. What was the place that you were taken in the first place?" Lauren wrote the name down, and then all the other stuff that she knew. It really wasn't much, but Lauren had worked with much less. "I'll see what I can dig up too. All right?"

"Yes, sure. I'm not sure if it's really my father, or some jackass pretending to be to take me in. I'm not going anywhere, but I could bring a world of shit down on you all." Lauren said that she would look forward to it. "I'm sure you would. But the others might not."

Lauren thought that they might not, but knew that they'd be on board with helping out. The McCulloughs were nothing if not dependable, and could gather their wagons around the family better than anyone that she'd ever met.

Frank—or Robert, as she'd found out about him—was still behind the dumpster. Lauren figured that it was pretty bad smelling too. It was ninety-four degrees out, and hotter than a brass bar in hell. Laughing again, she kept tabs on the cameras that had been put in the area as she looked for Jamie's father. She wanted to be her hero too, Lauren thought.

CHAPTER 12

Marshall didn't want to do it, but he was having no luck whatsoever finding his daughter by conventional means. So, he ran an ad in the paper that he was looking for anyone that might have been staying at the Our Lady of Trust between the years when he thought the child would have been dropped off. There wasn't a phone number with it—he'd set himself up an email account just for replies. Marshall and Gordon both figured they'd be inundated with them.

It was going to run for five days then stop. He'd then run it in some other town and see if he could get a hit there. It was a long shot, but one he was willing to wade through. He really wanted to find her.

"I've also called in a couple of favors on the dark web for you to have someone looking there. It might not be anyplace that would know, but as you said, we're getting down to the wire."

Marshall nodded and looked at the pictures on his desk. Four children, all of them boys, and not a one of them worth the sex it had taken to create them. Now they were trying to move him out of the company that he'd started when he'd been younger than them. His oldest, Michael, was the one pushing the hardest to have him retire. But Marshall just wasn't ready for that.

His son kept saying that he was the oldest and that he should be running the companies by now. What Michael really wanted to do was live off the money that came in every day. He'd no more know how to run the business than Marshall's wife would have when she'd been alive.

It wasn't the only reason that he wanted to find the girl — he supposed she'd be a woman now. It wasn't even a make or break kind of thing, hunting for her. He figured that he would retire eventually, but to have his daughter with him would be something that he could look forward to. Instead of hearing how his kids were fucking up the business.

"I have some information." He nearly screamed at Gordon to tell him, but Marshall calmly asked him what he'd found and Gordon smiled. "You did that very well, Marshall. I'm glad to see that you've not lost the ability to hide whatever you're feeling. But I have a lead. Strange though — it came in the form of an email I got before we ran the article in the paper."

"I'm a mess on the inside. I thought I'd practice a little before the board meeting in a couple of weeks. Those shits are going to try and convince the board that I'm not fit to work. I would love to have them say that I'm more than fit, but we'll see." Gordon told him he had this. "I hope so. What did you get from someone?"

"It's an email. And you're not going to believe who sent it. You remember about two years ago, that soldier that came back from overseas all busted to hell?" Marshall told him he

162

vaguely remembered something about it. "Her name back then was Sergeant Lauren Burcher. She's now called Major General McCullough. Ring any bells?"

"Yes. I had some dealings with a man by the name of McCullough. He had some property for sale and asked all kinds of questions before he would allow me to purchase it. I thought at the time he was insane or close to it, until I got a better look at the surrounding areas. He didn't want me to pollute the area for the others." Gordon told him that it was one and the same family. "What does this have to do with an email?"

Gordon handed him the printed email. He read it over twice before he put it down on his desk and let out long breaths. It was from Lauren McCullough all right, and she might know his daughter.

"How did she find out this information? Like your email address, for one thing?" Gordon told him that it came on his business email, which was public. "All right. I'd hate to think it was a scam, but you said that the papers hadn't run the article yet."

"No, and until we're able to check this out thoroughly, I stopped the paper from running anything. Just to be on the safe side." Marshall nodded and picked up the email again. "What do you want to do?"

"What do I want to do? I want to take off now for the little town that is mentioned, and find out if it's my child. But what I'm going to do is answer these questions that she put to you and hope for the best." Marshall felt his belly tighten up in nerves. "I like that she says she wants to be the hero in this. She's very careful not to give me too much information, but enough to pique my interest."

"I have no access to check this Lauren person out. Her files are sealed tighter than a virgin's legs on her first date. All I can tell you for sure about this woman is that she's married to a McCullough, has a job that gives her top-secret clearance, and she has the ear of the president. That one scares me a bit. For no other reason than I feel it, I think this woman is not one to screw around with."

Marshall wasn't really listening; he was reading over the missive again. "She wants to know where I'm working. I wonder why that's important. I mean, she could just look me up and find out that information, couldn't she?" He said that she might be making sure who was looking. "Could be, I suppose. But why all the cat and mouse things? You suppose there is a reason for that as well?"

"I haven't any idea, Marshall. I would suggest that you reply, using your personal email. You don't want this getting back to your sons. They'll have a heyday with it." They would too. Label him as crazy, searching for a long-lost child that may or may not be his. "When you email her, I'd be as upfront as you can be with her. Tell her all the reasons that you're looking, and why now. I think honesty is best for this situation."

"I'll do that."

He opened his computer just as his son walked in. Every time he saw his son, he wondered who his mother had been having an affair with. He looked nothing at all like either of them.

"What is it now, Jonas? In the event you didn't see it, I'm trying very hard to run my business here."

"For now. I was wondering if you've given any thought to my proposal to extend the line of credit to your secretary. It would help her getting her own supplies, as well as anything she needs without having to come to you for every cent." Marshall pulled up the file that had been dropped on his desk several days ago. "I'd like to give her an answer. I noticed that she's not here today. Is everything all right?"

"Oh yes, everything is wonderful. Tess has been fired. For misappropriation of company funds. And it's all because of you. Why? Weren't you getting enough money from me every month?" Jonas sat down. More like he flopped down in the chair with a pout on his lips. "What does your wife say about you having an affair with my secretary?"

"She doesn't care so long as I don't have any bastards, and that I'm not doing her in our bed." His son just smiled at him, like he had this big secret that no one else could guess. "Using this against me at the board meeting will do you no good. I know for a fact that three of your members are currently having an affair with someone in their offices. That would be hypocritical, don't you think?"

"Since we've taken care of Tess, why don't you go home or chase some other fool around their desk? I have things to do."

There was an envelope laid on his desk and his son winked at him. "There you go, Daddy Dear. The money that you owe the hotel that Tess and I stayed in when we were having a holiday. I do hope you won't wait too long to pay this. I would like to take someone else there soon. It's very romantic."

Jonas left them, and Marshall looked at Gordon. When he put out his hand, he handed him the envelope. They weren't paying the bills, none that had been dropped off to him over the last several months. All of his sons had been doing the same thing—treating him as if he were their own personal bank.

"I've changed the locks on the house as you've asked me to do. Also, the safe combination has been changed. There are new staff members there, and none of them are likely to help any of your sons by allowing them to come in and take what they want from now on." He thanked his friend. "I've also taken the liberty, I hope you don't mind, of having the cars removed from the property. I can't prove anything, but I do believe they were going to sell them off."

"More than likely. I saw an ad online just the other day that had a picture of my Jag on it. That's a priceless car, and he was selling it for ten grand. I nipped that in the bud as well." Gordon said that he'd make sure that there was a guard at the front gate from now on too. "Good thinking. Find someone that can't be bribed."

It had come to this, him having to hide his things from his sons. Otherwise they'd have sold everything that they could get their hands on. Some even if they couldn't. Jonas would sell his father's eyes if he thought he could make a dime off them.

Marshall worked until late in the evening. Gordon had come in several times over the day to tell him this bit of information or something. The email was all composed. All he needed to do was have Gordon look it over, so he could tell him if it sounded all right. As he was gathering up his coat and things, Gordon came in and read it over for him. Then Jonas came in the door with his brothers. All three of them.

"Dad, you've gone too far now." Marshall asked him what he'd done that had them so upset. "There is a man at the front gate to our home that isn't allowing any of us to come

166

on the property. He said that you told him specifically that he wasn't to allow us to come in. Why would you do that to us?"

"Several reasons. And the fact that I have to explain them to you shows me that this is the best thing I've done since you demanded your first bit of money from me." David sat in the chair while Jonas paced. Chad wasn't saying much, but of all his kids, Chad was the one that he was afraid of. He had an evilness about him that frankly scared Marshall. Michael was sitting on the side of his desk, something that they all knew he hated. "You'll not be running in and out of here anymore after today either. I've put in fresh guards at the door and gate with the same instructions. Also, I'd be careful where you charge things from now on. Your credit cards have been cut off."

"You're playing with fire here, old man. You should know better than to treat us like we're nothing to you." It was on the tip of his tongue to tell Chad that they had become nothing to him when he heard his computer ding. Pushing it to Gordon to deal with, he waited for his boys to have their say. "What do you think this is going to accomplish? You'll be out on your ass in a few days. What are you going to do then? Nothing. You'll regret this."

"No more than I do now that I've had to come to this with you four." He sat down in his chair. "Anything else you'd like to tell me? I do have a busy night ahead of me."

David asked about his order for new shoes. They were being held up for non-payment. Michael said that he had been told the same thing about his four new suits. Marshall laughed. It felt good to get this confrontation over with. It wasn't finished, but he was glad that they knew what steps he'd made to take away the things they liked most. Whatever money could buy them.

"As I said, the cards have been cut off. And as of yesterday, all companies that you've dealt with have been informed that I will not pay the bills. Nor will you be able to have lavish parties in places that you have destroyed — unless, of course, you have the funds to pay for it. I'm finished with the lot of you." He stood up again, his knees somewhat shaky. "Now, I think it's about time that you left here. It doesn't matter if you leave your badges or not. They've all been disabled as of the moment you used them to get in here tonight."

As they were leaving, Chad swiped everything off his desk with a swipe. Then he stood and laughed as he crushed the things that hadn't broken with his boots. Michael went to the liquor cabinet and broke several of the glasses there. Lucky for him, Marshall had had the liquor taken out days ago. David took out a knife, and for a moment, Marshall thought that he was going to use it on him. But he only sliced up the couch with it before coming toward the chairs that they'd been sitting in. But Jonas beat him to them, picking them up and tossing them across the room toward the windows. They wouldn't break, thankfully, or he might have found himself hurtling through the air to the ground floor.

Security walked in just as they were starting on the file cabinets.

"It's time to go." They were armed, his new security team, and he was glad to see that each of them had their hands on their weapons, and they were ready to be pulled and fired. "We'll see you out."

"I'm not leaving until he gives us what we want." The security guard told Jonas that whatever it was, he'd taken it by destroying the office. When his son looked at him, he could see an anger in his eyes that had him holding his breath. "You'll regret this. See if you don't."

He sat down with a heavy sigh when they were gone. Marshall's hands were shaking so badly that he sloshed water all over the desk as he held the glass of it from his friend. Gordon stood by him until he was all right again.

"They threatened you, Marshall. Not once, but several times." He said that he'd caught that too. "Oh, by the way, you hit send on the email before I came in. Must have been fat fingers. Anyway, it sounded good. I'm glad you told her everything that you knew. It might lead to nothing, but you can never tell about this sort of thing."

Marshall prayed all the way to his limo that this was his daughter. And that she could stand up to the men that his sons had become. But his luck would be that she was no different than them and just as money hungry as the rest of them. He supposed time would tell him.

~*~

Hawkins read the email four times. Now all he had to do was tell Jamie. Lauren said his name, and he was sure that she'd said it more than once. When she smiled at him, he felt the dread of telling Jamie all over again.

"She'll either answer him or not. What will it do to her if we find out that this guy is as off his rocker as Webley was? Remember that crackpot? That guy was fucking nuts all the way to his core." Hawkins said he was good under pressure, though. "Yes, he was at that. Most of the time I would send him in first to see if anyone else would think he was as loony as we thought he was."

"He was a part of that restaurant bombing, wasn't he?" Lauren nodded, her smile gone. They had lost five men that day. Good men who only wanted a hot meal that didn't come out of a bag. "You don't think she'll be upset that we went ahead and talked to him without talking to her?"

"No, I don't. When we were talking the other day, she seemed as if she didn't give a shit if this man was her father or not. She thinks it might have been a cover to capture her, but I don't think so. She wants this to be over with one way or the other." That's pretty much what he'd gotten from Jamie. That if he was her father, she didn't care. He'd not spent any time in her life. And if he was, it was too little too late.

"This email, it's very telling, don't you think? I mean, he's very forthcoming about what he thinks of a good reason to find her, as well as how he found out about her. This will make a difference to her, I think."

Hawkins didn't want her hurt.

When he'd found the name of the man who owned the building currently, it wasn't difficult to discover from there that the same person was also searching for anyone that might have been there a long time ago. He got up to look out the window into the yard. The office out here in the barn was massive, and ran with the utmost high quality equipment. Lauren used it to help the president, and the family when they needed it as well. It was small wonder that Lauren had been able to track him down. She had access to every kind of database there was, he thought.

"I'm going to look for his sons. Just to see what sort of people they are. I'm betting that they're little goody two shoes that wouldn't hurt a fly, and probably wear real pennies in their loafers." Lauren thought that was an excellent idea, and he could hear her fingers running over the keyboard. At her loud whistle, he turned and asked her what she'd unearthed.

"Holy shit, Hawkins. These men are the cream of the crop, and I don't mean that in a good way. They're fucking nuts."

"How so?" She told him what she'd found in only the first search. It was about one called Chad. "So, they went to a wedding that they'd not been invited to and destroyed the cake? Why, does it say?"

"Because he could, according to this reporter. It also says that there were four men there that night, all of them Penningtons, that trashed the reception so badly that it had to be moved to another venue. They did several thousand dollars' worth of damage, as well as took the wedding limo out for a joy ride and wrecked it too. Nothing was done to them, apparently, because their father, Marshall Pennington, paid everyone for their crimes. But this reporter says that he saw the elder gentleman sobbing for what had been done."

"Do you think that he pays everyone off every time one of them gets into trouble?" Lauren didn't answer him, and he walked back to where she was sitting. Reading the article over her shoulder, Hawkins noticed that it was dated yesterday. He asked her to wait for him to catch up before she scrolled down. After they both read it, he sat down in the chair beside her desk. "He's cut them off. Not only that, but he's had to put in extra security, as well as changing locks on the doors to his homes and businesses. Why would someone put that in the paper?"

"To let the world know that he is finished with them. Not only that, but as you read, he's not going to be responsible for anything that they do, destroy, or steal. I guess that's been a major issue as well." Hawkins just shook his head. "This attorney, I've decided to give him a call. Just to see if this shit in on the up and up."

171

"Don't." She asked him why. "I don't know. Let me talk to Jamie first, and then we'll go from there. I don't want to keep her in the dark of all this that we have so far. She needs to know where we are and what we've found out. She knows that we're looking, she just doesn't know how far we've gotten."

After asking for all the information that Lauren had unearthed, he gathered it all up and started for the door. He was standing there, just half way in and out, when he looked at Lauren. He had so much on his mind now that he wasn't sure where to start with it all. Turning around but not leaving his position, he realized that this was how he'd felt about being home. In and out of it.

"When we get this figured out about her dad or whoever he is, I'm going to take Jamie on an extended trip. Not a vacation, but a trip to see all the places I've been without her. I want to see them again through her eyes and not mine." Lauren nodded. He thought that of all people, she'd understand. "I'm sleeping through the night now. No nightmares where I wake up with a gun in my hand, sweaty, in the dark. I've stopped writing in the journals and have been eating better. And it's all because of her. I cannot, nor will I ever be able to, explain to her what it was like there. And to be honest, I don't want to. When I think of all the things I've done in the name of justice, I want to sit in a corner and hide."

"I do understand, Hawkins. And I can feel your pain. Without your brother loving me the way that he does, I think I'd be right there with you, sucking my thumb. But, we're both all right. A little beat to fuck, and have a few issues with stupid people, but we have someone that loves us, and an entire clan to lean on when we need it." Hawkins nodded but

172

didn't move. "What else is it?"

"I'm finished, for real. I don't want to be called on to take someone out anymore, to steal back something that the government wants. Nor do I want to be on alert all the time, like I'm just waiting for someone to try and kill me." He grinned at her. "Okay, the last part might be harder to do, but I'm done working like this. I'm going to be a father, and I'd like to be there for him. I need that."

Feeling better that he'd told her, Hawkins went out of the big barn, which had nothing at all to do with livestock or hay, and made his way to his truck. His plan today was to meet his dad and brothers in town and help work on the houses that they had lined up. But he had to talk to Jamie first.

He told Dad where he was going and what he was going to do, and that he would see him later today.

You go on now and tell that girl all you know. She has a level head on those pretty shoulders of hers, and she'll do just fine with the information, whatever it is. He told him a little about what they'd learned. *Well then, you tell her that we love her, and if she don't want to go through with this, then that's all right too. We'll take good care of her.*

Hawkins told his dad that he knew that, and was sure that she did as well. Making his way home, he just hoped that he was right—that she'd not care a whit, as Dad said, and that she'd be just as fine as rain when it came to this family. But in his heart, he knew that meeting her family was going to be harder on her than she was letting on. If she wanted to, that is.

Pulling in the drive, he saw her in the back yard. He had no idea what she was doing, but watched her. She was, simply put, a beauty and a wonder to him. Getting out of the truck, he watched as she turned into her flame and reached out to different trees on the land. She was clear cutting, he realized, and laughed all the way to her. She was very useful too, he thought.

"I have some news for you." She cooled herself off and kissed him. He noticed that Jon was with her too. "It's about your father and his family. Do you want to talk about it?"

"Not right now, if you don't mind. Jon and I are seeing if, together, we are a bigger force. Sadly, we're not able to connect that way. It would have been fun to share some of this with him, I think."

Hawkins wasn't sure that he could handle any more power from her, but laughed when Jon pouted. The way he spoke and acted all the time, a person could forget that he was just a kid that had been dealt a nasty blow. Same with Jamie.

"Later then. Whenever you're ready. I'm going to go into town and work for a bit with my dad and the rest of them. If you change your mind, let me know and I'll come here. All right?" Jamie nodded and kissed him again before he left.

He was all right without telling her now. In fact, he was glad for it, for now anyway. Hawkins wanted all the details that he could gather before he was asked questions that he couldn't answer. So, asking Lauren to give him all she found as she found it and why he wanted it, he lifted the first sheet of dry wall after getting to the house site.

Chapter 13

Jamie read over everything that she'd been handed. Lauren had called her about an hour after Jon left her and before lunch. Walking over there — it wasn't really that far — she thought about what she'd been told so far about her father and her half-brothers. They didn't sound like people that she'd like to meet anyway.

But she would meet them. It was what she knew that she should do. Perhaps she wasn't his daughter and he was chasing ghosts, but there was a tiny chance, at least in her heart, that she might be. When she got to the fence line that separated their lands, she paused to look around.

It was beautiful back here in the deeper part of the woods. It was cooler too, and the animals, when you paused long enough, were more plentiful than they were anyplace else. There were wolves running around, and she knew that some of them were shifters, while the rest were natural born wolves. She envied them in that they could blend in so well with similar creatures. She wasn't like anyone she had ever met.

175

The birds were singing and making a loud noise, singing a song that made her feel lighter, her heart quieter, and her soul more complete. Sitting on a nearby rock, she watched the animals at play, foraging for food and simply lying in the rays of sun that streamed their way through the dense trees.

There were deer and wolves aplenty, but there was also a family of raccoons out taking in the sights. A leash of foxes seemed to be as cautious as the raccoons, but neither of them bothered with the other. It was as if they felt no need to use their differences of prey and meal while in this area of the forest.

As the animals got used to her being there, more of them ventured out of their homes. Birds were pecking at trees for a meal, while turtles popped their heads out and stretched their necks to get the juiciest green leaves. There were butterflies and insects too, their beauty only rivaled by the rainbows that danced over the stream when the sunlight, seldom showing itself here, peeked through the trees just a little.

Jamie sat there, watching the animals as families, each of them feeling the same thing that she was as she sat there. A sense of peace. A feeling of calmness. And the love of family. All things that she'd never dreamed of having while she'd been all alone in the world. Then her thoughts turned to her father.

Whether or not he was the real deal or not, she wondered why he wanted her in his life so badly. Did he want to sell her off? She didn't think so. When reading the things that she'd been given this afternoon by a courier that Lauren had sent, she thought him to be lonelier than she had been. And just as unloved. Perhaps, she thought, she could help him as the McCulloughs had her.

Getting up quietly, she finished her walk to Lauren's to help her with a project and to catch up on the information that she'd been able to find. She hadn't been sure that it was anything that she wanted — information on a man that she neither knew nor had any connection with. The fact that she might or might not be his child didn't play into the fact that he was a troubled man.

Walking into the building with Lauren, she knew what she had to do. But the moment that she stepped inside, she knew that something else had happened.

"It seems that your half-brothers — if they are relatives at all — have decided that they don't care for the way that your possible father has finally gotten his ball out of the jar and started to make them adults." She asked if he'd been killed. "No, but not for lack of trying on their part. They ran him off the road when he was out jogging, and then came back and beat him with a blunt object. I'm thinking bat."

"Why would they do that to their own father?" Lauren told her that people had done more for less. "I suppose. But it doesn't make it right. I'm not naïve enough to think that it never happens, but it seems to be happening more and more, don't you think? Don't answer that. Tell me, honestly, what would you do now?"

"Honestly, I have no idea. But I do know that I would like to know for sure if he's my father or not. I have a pretty great one now, but my biological parents were dirt. And I mean that literally. They lived in trash, treated me like trash, and were never good role models. I have a wonderful mother and father now, a little brother that I love more than I can explain, and someone that I can lean on when the going gets tough." Jamie told her that she had heard about how the Burchers had

177

found her. "Yes, they saved my life that night too. Had it not been for them taking me in, I wouldn't be alive today. I know that. Someone else might have found me, and I wasn't as mean as I am now. They would have done all kinds of things to me, then killed me and dumped me in an unmarked hole someplace."

Jamie wandered around the room. There was more equipment in this one place than she'd seen in a well-stocked computer store, or even a warehouse full of this stuff. While she didn't know what it was all used for, Jamie knew that Lauren and even Hawk used it for their other jobs. Running her fingers over the computer screen in front of her, she spoke to Lauren.

"When I was first taken to the lab, they told me that I'd meet my parents and that they'd take very good care of me. I didn't have a clue what that meant—no one had taken care of me since I was old enough to understand what caring for someone actually meant." She moved to another piece of shiny equipment, and just looked at it without really seeing it. "My family, as they called them, was a bunch of men in white lab coats that wore guns on their hips like one would a stethoscope around their neck. I was terrified at first, not having a clue what was going on. But then one night, after they had injected me with several different things that day, I realized that I had abilities that I'd not had before."

"You showed them, didn't you?" Jamie nodded and moved around the room again. "They were thrilled, I take it."

"Oh yes. They celebrated like it was Christmas and they'd gotten everything that they wanted on their list. But I was locked away in a cage, in the same room with them, as they ate roast beef sandwiches, drank champagne, and ate cake."

Lauren no longer mattered to her. Jamie's mind had gone back to that day like she was there still. "Cake. I wanted a piece of that cake so badly that I was drooling for it. And when I started crying, wailing for a piece of anything, they banged on the cage and told me to shut up, that their celebration was being ruined by my pettiness."

"I'm sorry." Jamie waved Lauren off. While she hadn't been able to do anything then, she had made sure that they didn't know another thing about what she'd accomplished. "What made you stay there if you could have, at any time, left? If you don't mind me asking."

"Where was I to go? The only places I knew were the orphanage and the lab. There was nothing in between. And as far as I knew, they were all like the people that I'd encountered thus far." Lauren told her she was sorry again. "Don't. But I've also been thinking about this man and his claim that I may be his daughter. I want to go through with whatever it takes to find out. Do you know what I need to do?"

"Yes. I can contact his attorney and let him know first. Then we'll take you to Mackenzie or Boyd and get your DNA tested. I can run it for you in less than twenty-four hours." Jamie told her to do it. "All right. Let me send this email first. He might say no, and there is no point in going farther if he's not going to play ball."

"Do you think he'll say no?" Lauren just smiled at her. "Yeah, I don't think he will either. And for some reason—and I haven't really given it a great deal of thought on the pros and cons of this—but if it turns out I'm not his daughter, I'm going to help him anyway with his sons. I don't know how yet, but I want to."

"Good. I was hoping you'd say that. But before you meet

179

the idiots that might be related to you, how about you and I take a trip? Just to the hospital that Mr. Pennington is at. It won't take long to get there. He is out of recovery now, and should be able to talk to you before too much longer." Jamie asked her if she thought that was a good idea. "I do. And I've already spoken to Hawkins, and he's going too."

"Then why are you going? Not that I don't want you to, but I'm curious." She told her. "I don't think they'll hurt me. I'm stronger than all of them put together. Even smarter, I'd bet."

"Oh yeah, you are at that. But I'm going to keep you from hurting them. Because they have hit the top of my shit list. Honey, I don't even want to get into how many people are on that list, and how many idiots they have passed to get to the top." Jamie laughed. It felt good after her talk with Lauren. "Okay, Hawkins is on his way, as is a DNA test for you to take now. Then we'll get going the minute he gets here. I have the nanny here all day in case I had to go out again. This will be fun. Or not. I don't care at this point."

Hawkins seemed to be as thrilled about this as Jamie was apprehensive. There was so much that could go wrong with this. She may not like Mr. Pennington. He could be an asshole. Then again, he could be the sweetest man on earth that had simply been duped. Not just by his sons, but her mother as well, in what she'd done to him in the first place concerning her.

Getting in the truck with the other two, she wondered if she was making the biggest mistake of her life. No, she thought, that would have been being in the lab for so long. This, seeing a man who she didn't know, that was child's play after the life she had led. But the men that were his children needed a swift kick in the ass, and she wasn't going to take any bullying from them.

Reaching for the rest of the things that Lauren had, Jamie read over the other stuff as well. It wasn't a long drive to Columbus, but it seemed to go faster because she stayed busy and focused on what she was doing.

By the time they were parked, she was all butterflies and snakes. Yes, she thought to herself, it was a strange combination, but she was almost making herself ill with this. Jamie thought that she might have liked to have stayed home and looked for Jackson. At least there, she knew he was a bad guy and needed taken out. Jamie darted in the gift shop when she just needed a moment. No one came in after her, but Hawkins did reach out to her.

Are you okay with this? We don't have to do this now. She told Hawkins that she knew that, but she really wanted to get it over with. *His attorney took a swab of his mouth too, so as soon as the lab is finished with them, you should know. Lauren is rushing it.*

What if he is my father? I don't know what I'm supposed to do with that information. Do I tell him what was done to me? Do I show him? I know that I'm stretching into territory that might not matter, but I'm terrified out of my gore with this. He laughed and told her that if they gave her any shit, to burn the lot of them. *You jest about that, but I might have to after what I read about those boys of his.*

And we'll cross that bridge when we get to it, if we ever do. What we're doing today is going to see a gentleman at his request. Nothing more needs to be read into it until we're as sure as shit about it. And trust me when I tell you, I've known Lauren for a couple of decades, and she'll make sure that this is the real deal. Again, if it comes to that.

181

Jamie came out of the gift shop with a small planter of flowers. It said simply "Get well soon," without a name on it. "Are you ready now? And I love that you thought of flowers. It might be something that he won't get from anyone else. Especially his sons."

"They're going to require me to kick their asses, I'm sure of it. If they get wind that I might be their half-sister, this is going to be a war." Hawkins told her that he wasn't worried. He had the two bravest and strongest women with him, and they'd come out on top. "You say that now, but I might be in prison before this is done."

They knocked on the door and were told to come in. Mr. Pennington didn't know they were coming here, and the attorney told Lauren that was where he was to have the test done. As soon as she walked in the door, she realized how wrong she'd been about the flowers. As well as the man on the bed. He looked nothing like the person she'd been dreaming of coming for her, but a man like any other.

"Oh my God." Jamie looked behind her when Mr. Pennington sat up more on the bed. "You're her. You're my daughter. I can't believe how much you— Gordon, show her the picture of Becky." He just kept staring at her until Jamie felt uncomfortable. But when the other man handed her a picture, she gave it to Hawkins without looking. "I'm glad that you're here. I've been trying to find you since I was informed of you. You're very beautiful. Jamie—they said that your name is Jamie."

"It's James, actually. When I was dropped off at the orphanage there was a blank birth certificate on my blanket. The guy that found me—he was the gardener or something— didn't check my gender and put James in the blank lines. I was dressed all in blue, as it turns out. As he worked outside and didn't see me at all, it wasn't until several months later that it was discovered that he'd made a mistake. He had filed the certificate on his way home from work that day." Mr. Pennington laughed, then had to hold his head while he laid back on the bed. "I don't know what to do or what you expect of me."

"Neither do I, but I'm so glad to meet you, James Pennington Fitzpatrick McCullough." This time it was all of them that laughed, then Hawkins handed her the old photo.

"Holy fuck, I do look like her."

Marshall talked to Jamie for as long as he was allowed. He was so pleased that she was upfront about everything he'd asked her, but not what she'd done after she'd been adopted out from Our Lady of Trust. He wanted to ask her outright, but really, he was afraid of knowing. There was something odd about all of them, and then it hit him.

"Shifters. You're all shifters." He looked at Jamie as he continued. "But you. You're not like them, are you? I'm not saying that you're different in a bad way, but you're human, aren't you? That's what I meant to say." Jamie looked at Hawkins and Lauren, and they both left the room. "Whatever you're going to tell me, I'm not going to like it, am I?"

"I haven't any idea if you will or not, to be honest. I had thought before coming here that you might have been a part of what happened to me, but now I can see that you didn't know." She got up to look out the window, and Marshall was astonished again at how much she looked like her birth mother. "I wasn't adopted, as you've been told, but sold to a laboratory not far from here. They used me for a test rat for about ten years or so. I escaped not long after another one like me was able to."

"I don't understand." She nodded as if she knew that he'd not. "Can you make me understand, Jamie? I want to know what these men did to you. Because as surely as I'm here laid up, they're going to be in worse shape."

"You don't have to do that. They're all dead or in jail. Lauren and her team took them out." Jamie looked at him then. "She and Hawkins are working for the government, and have been for over twenty years. I can't tell you what they did or are doing, but they've been on missions that you'd not want to hear about anyway."

"I see." But he didn't, not really. "But this lab, you said that they tested things on you. I'm assuming that it wasn't how sugar affects your brain." She shook her head and put out her hand. He reached for it, thinking that she wanted to hold his, when a bright white fire appeared. "Holy Moses. That's fire. Is it burning you?"

"No. It never burns me." She was suddenly and profoundly covered in the same flame that had been in her hand. And through it all, she spoke to him as if it were nothing for this to be happening. "I have other talents as well. I can manipulate someone's computer. Back search from a touch who the person touched, and then from there, see who they might have come in contact with. There are many more, but I think that's enough for you for now, correct?"

"Yes. I'm slightly overwhelmed right now. I'm intrigued, but also overwhelmed. I'd like to be able to help you out of this." She told him that it was as much a part of her now as his blood and skin were to him. "So this is only some of the many things that were done to you there."

"It is. There was another there—well, more than just the two of us—that they experimented on. The young man that I was the guinea pig for, he's my nephew by marriage now. And he's like me, but much less on the scale of scary shit." He nodded and smiled at her. "You try and sell me off to some lab, and they'll never find your body."

"No. No, I'd never do anything like that. Never. My sons might. I just realized that they're your half-brothers. You won't like them. I certainly don't." She laughed, and he was reminded of his own mother's laughter. She laughed all the time when he'd been a child. "Please, have a seat and talk to me. I've missed so much of your life that I find that I want to know every bit of it. Even the bad parts. Please?"

"Not today. I can see that you're exhausted—there is straining around your eyes." He was feeling each cut and bruise on his body. "I'll come back tomorrow, and we can talk then. But don't expect anything from me just yet. I'm only just now getting used to being around people again. And I'm not going to change myself to suit you either. If we are related, you take me as I am."

"I'd be honored to let you be what you are." He watched her stand, and then she looked around the room. "I'm well liked. If you'd like to talk to some of the people that I work with at Pennington Corp, I can arrange that for you too."

"Let's not go putting the cart before the horse. One step at a time." He nodded and told her goodbye when she left him. "I'll be back tomorrow unless Lauren needs me. My job working with her has to come first." Then she left him.

Marshall sat there for a long time, deep in thought. Then he reached for his phone and snatched his hand back when it rang first. It was Gordon, just the man that he needed to speak

185

with.

"She's your daughter, Marshall. She hits all the markers, the report said, and she's ninety-nine-point-nine percent a Pennington." Marshall started to cry. He had a daughter. After all this time, he had himself a little girl. "I'm guessing that she's left you by now. I like her, by the way, and her husband. He's a good man, and a very wealthy one. More so than you are by a large margin."

"Good for them. They have been through a great deal. She didn't tell me it all, but she's been abused. More than I could have imagined when I started this search." Gordon told him that Hawkins had told him some. "I want you to come in here. Bring that secretary of yours in. I have something I need for you to do. Have you heard from the bane of my life today?"

When Marshall had told Jamie that he didn't like his sons, he'd not been lying. But it was the first time that he'd said it aloud, and he felt very good about disliking them. It hadn't been him that had given them everything that they'd wanted, it had been his wife. And when she'd died, they expected the same kind of treatment from him.

Marshall had done it for a little while, about a month. Then he realized what horrible people they were. Little by little he'd started cutting them off, until the other day when he'd had enough. That had cost him too. They had nearly killed him when he'd been out jogging.

"I did hear from Chad. I think the others were with him. He told me that I wasn't going to be their attorney when you were dead if I didn't start playing ball with them. I just hung up. Sometimes it's better to cut that crap off before it gets out of hand. And to be honest, I wouldn't work for them even if you begged me to." Marshall said that he'd never do that to him. "I know that, Marshall. These boys, men really, have had this coming for a long time. It was Rachel's fault, indulging them in every whim until it was expected from you. I'm glad that you're doing something about this. And Clark and I will be in shortly. I'll bring you what I've been able to find out about Jamie, and her new family as well."

While waiting on his attorney, he made notes of things that he wanted done. He was sure that Jamie had the results — she might even have had them while talking to him. But he knew now, and was going to make some changes to his life. For her. He wanted to devote as much as he could to her now that he'd found her. Marshall was glad that the meeting for the board had been put off for a few more days while he recovered. He wondered if his sons knew that because of what they'd done, they were delayed in trying to kick him out of his own company.

By the time Gordon and Clark showed up, he had a long list of things that he wanted done. And he also had a list of things that he wanted to speak to Jamie about. His daughter. Marshall couldn't believe how much pleasure it gave him to say that. Marshall thought of all the things that were going to happen, and the order in which he would like to see them happen. But he needed this done first. And he needed to talk to Jamie and Hawkins. He was going to ask them to help him out of this situation with his sons.

"God, I hope this will work." He asked Gordon, when he'd read over his list, if he thought it might. "I don't know, but I'd say that it will. Lauren told me that Jamie wanted to help you out with them even before she'd met you. So, she's going to help you, I know it."

187

"Good. And the other things? You can take care of them before this meeting of the minds, so to speak?" Gordon assured him that he would have it all done before tomorrow morning. "I want you to be careful around them. They're not finished with me yet. And I'd just as soon you weren't hurt by them."

"I've hired us bodyguards. Hawkins is going to keep an eye on both of us for the time being. There is a man outside your door right now that I'd not want to mess with. His name is Bear. I think he's actually a bear too. And Hawkins is with me until this is resolved." Marshall nearly cried again. He was emotional, he knew that, and blamed it on the pain and the medication. "Marshall, I'm very glad that you've done this. I wasn't at first, I'll be honest with you. But now that you've found her and have taken steps to cut those mongrels off, I'm very happy to be helping you."

"I am as well, my friend. I am as well. And by this time Friday, we should all be happy about the way things will go. At least I hope we will."

Gordon assured him they would, but Marshall wasn't as sure. He'd been disappointed for too long now to give up on that. His sons were not going to be happy. And Marshall thought he might do a little jig. After he was feeling more himself, that was.

CHAPTER 14

Jamie stood outside the big meeting room and paced. There was a great deal riding on this today, and she didn't want to fuck this up for Marshall. He'd been kind to her the last few days, and even brought her pictures of her biological mother. She knew more about her now than she'd ever thought she would. And Marshall told her things about his life too, so she'd be caught up, as he called it.

"Are you ready for this?" She smiled at Hawkins and he grinned at her. "These men aren't going to know what hit them, are they? I love it. You might be a bigger mercenary than me, my dear wife."

They'd gotten officially married yesterday morning. All his brothers and sisters-in-law were in attendance, as well as his parents, Gordon, and Marshall. She glanced down at the beautiful ring that he'd slipped on her finger when they'd been proclaimed man and wife. Jamie had never been happier to have a name change than she'd been yesterday. Gordon had come to witness the marriage for the board if they asked. Marshall had come because at the last minute, Rich had told

189

her that she should ask her father to give her away. He'd been so happy to take the job that Marshall had cried while holding her hand.

The little buzzer sounded, and she took a deep breath. This was going to help a man that she'd come to admire and to like a great deal. She went to the door and let her breath out slowly, then turned the knobs to let herself in. The entire room stood up when she stepped in, except for the four men she was here to usurp.

"Have a seat please." She leaned down and kissed Marshall on the top of his bald head, then sat down in the chair next to him, pulling one from the wall to be closer to him than his sons. "My name is Jamie McCullough. I've recently found out that Marshall Pennington is my biological father." The room was so silent that she could hear the air conditioning running.

"Oh, hell no." One of the sons stood up and Marshall told her it was Chad. "You are not going to come in here and make a claim like that. Get the fuck out of here."

Jamie stood as well, knowing that the way they treated her from now on depended on what she did at this moment. Walking to the end of the table, where Chad was, Jamie drew back and slugged him right in the face. Then she calmly and quietly sat down again.

"If there are no more objections to my being here, then I'd like for this meeting to proceed." One of the others stood up, and this one was David. He made his way to her, but before he could get to her, Hawkins drew his gun and held it at his side. Laughing, she looked at the other two. "You, any of you, get up again before this meeting is over, and I will personally see that you're bleeding before you can make a sound."

"You're all bad assed when you have a guard standing

there with a gun out. And I thought that guns weren't allowed in this place." She was told this was Michael. "I'm thinking of calling the police and having them remove him. Then we'll see what you have to say for yourself."

"If you think you can hurt her, then by all means give it your best shot. You fight dirty and I will take over. But, as I said, have at it." Hawkins backed away, handing his weapon to Gordon. "For safekeeping, and so that you know that I'm not going to interfere with her taking you all down."

Michael stood up, and so did the other three. Jamie did the same and waited for them to come near her. As soon as she could touch one of them, Michael again, she grabbed him around the throat and tossed him across the room. Chad was next. All she did was hit him in the face, twice, before picking up a chair and putting it across his chest and sat on it so that he couldn't move. David tried to knock her off, or it seemed that he was trying something anyway. Jamie remained where she was and slammed her fist into his belly. Then, standing for the briefest of moments, she kicked him in the balls. And she didn't hold back on her powers, either.

"You coming to try and hurt me, Jonas, or are you going to be a good boy and have a seat and shut the fuck up?" She looked down at the man under the chair, and put her foot on his throat when he started screaming at her. "Shut the fuck up."

The room was quiet except for the moans of the other two. Jamie looked around the room and then back at Chad. He wasn't all that scary now, she thought, but she knew that this wouldn't end here.

"Now, I'm going to allow you to stand up, but you even think about fucking with me and I'll end you. Not a threat either—I will simply ram your nose bones right into that small brain of yours, and even if you were in the hospital when it happened, there would be no saving you."

"Who the fuck are you?" She told Michael that she was his half-sister. "Not so long as I'm alive you're not. I'm the oldest here, and you will heel to me."

"Heel? Did you seriously just say that? I'm not a dog, you moronic fuck, but a woman. And one that just mopped the floor with your ass and two more, with only having a single one of you touch me." Chad started cursing and she put her foot back over his neck, and put the littlest bit of pressure on him. "You are going to listen to me, or so help me, you'll die right here. And I'm thinking that there isn't a soul here that will give any fuck about it. Isn't that right?"

The men around the table nodded, each of them telling her that they were glad someone had stood up to them. She let Chad speak, and Jamie laughed as she stood and removed the chair to let him up.

She was fully prepared for him to come at her. What she hadn't counted on was him having a knife. And when he slashed out with it, nicking her arm, the gun went off and no one moved when Chad fell to the floor, holding his knife hand.

True to what he had threatened, Hawkins had shot him. He didn't kill him, though he might yet as the anger in his face seemed to reach out and touch her. She put her hand on Hawkins's shoulder and had him look at her.

"I'm all right, I promise you. And I think you made your point quite well." He winked at her, then kissed her on the mouth. She looked around the room and then at Marshall. "Are you all right? Did you get hurt in this?"

"Hurt? Hell no, I'm not hurt. But I think I made the right decision yesterday." Marshall stood up and cleared his throat. "Gentlemen, I'd like you to meet my daughter, Jamie McCullough. I'd stay on her good side if I were you. She's going to be taking over my job when I retire. In the meantime, I'm going to be training her on how to run this place."

Marshall was laughing as he left the room. The security team came in then and escorted his four sons out of the room. Jamie sat down then and looked at Hawkins, who was grinning from ear to ear about something. When she glanced at Gordon, who told her that he needed her signature, she signed it without reading it. This was just too bizarre to get straight in her head right now. As the others left, telling her their names and that they were glad she was taking over, she looked at Hawkins when it was just the two of them in the room.

"What just happened? I thought I was here just to put his sons in their place. What did they mean when they congratulated me on being here? I'm not staying." Hawkins told her that he thought for sure that she was. "No, I don't want to run a company. I can barely run my own life, much less this.... What the hell does this business do, anyway?"

Hawkins was laughing harder than she'd ever seen him when he left her sitting at the long table. The longer that she sat there, going over each thing that had happened, she realized that she'd signed something and not read it. Jamie got up to find Gordon and tell him that she wanted the paperwork back that she'd signed, that she'd changed her mind.

"I'm afraid that you can't do that, Miss Jamie. I've already filed the paperwork that states that you're taking over the company, and will be staying on after Marshall is gone.

Which won't be long, I'm afraid. He has an advanced form of cancer." She had just found him, damn it. "I'm sorry. But he was so happy to find out that you might be out there and that you were his daughter. I have to tell you, neither of us knew what to expect from you. But I should tell you that neither of us thought you'd be so good at keeping them in line."

"But he's more their father than mine." He asked her if she'd been in the room when all that shit was going on. "Yes. Well, I was showing off a little."

"Be that as it may, you made an impression on both of us, Marshall and I, as well as the board. All of them were ready to bail if any of the boys had been made president and CEO of the company." She asked him what the company did. "They go into areas that have been stripped of all that made it a forest or town and rebuild. Housing, as well as other things that a family might need. There are trees planted, as well as gardens are put in. That's not all we do—we also help with the design of equipment for people that might need something. Like a new leg because the one that they have has been broken or stolen. The moneymaker, however, the one that allows us to make these incredible donations, are the products that we make and distribute all over the world. We make Marshall Chocolates. Named after Marshall's dad, who made the confections right here on this property before it was built up. We're very famous for that and a line of wines that we grow the grapes for, as well as cheeses from the dairy farms that we have that are run by good people who take care of—"

Jamie cut him off by simply raising her hand. Gordon gave her a file and a copy of today's newspaper. He left her when she picked it up. On the front page was an article stating how Marshall Pennington had found his long-lost daughter, and that she was going to take over the running of his businesses. She was deep in reading it when Lauren joined her.

"You'll do a great job." Jamie told her that she didn't think so. "Yes. Well, you tamed the beast inside of Hawkins—you can do about anything you set your mind to, I think. Running this size of a business will be a piece of cake for you. I have the go ahead with Jackson. Are you ready to help us end this shit?"

"Yes. I can help you. Whatever you need for me to do." Lauren said that she didn't know what just yet, but she wanted her there in the event it all went to shit. "You never have things go to shit that you don't fix before anyone knows about it."

"That is true. I'm very good at thinking on my feet. And so are you. That is why you and I are going to be an awesome duo, or perhaps the biggest dumb asses on the plant." Jamie told her that she didn't think that was going to be possible; she thought that her brothers had that all sewn up. "Yes, you might have a point there. Let's go and take in Jackson and have a nice dinner in town before going home. You have a busy week in front of you."

Jamie wasn't sure, but she thought that Lauren was enjoying this too much. But she went with her. This really did have to end with this man. He needed to be taken care of so that others could sleep at night.

.⌣*.⌣

Jackson was sick and tired of not being able to take his plan to the next level. There were road blocks all the way around every little thing that he tried to get going. Like his money and the fact that he couldn't get to it. The woman on the phone had been less than helpful, and he'd wanted to go and strangle her when she told him that the money was gone. But she didn't have any idea why. Mother fuck, there was a lot of money in that account, and someone was fucking with him.

He made his way to the diner, checking his costume as he went. The place was busy, as it usually was. Frank was able to snag a booth when two people got up to leave. Tonight's special was roast beef. Not that it was that tasty or anything, but it had grown on him, the way the cook made things. The waitress brought him a cup of black water mistaken as coffee, and a little pitcher of cream.

"You want the special tonight?" He didn't even glace up at the woman, but told her that was fine. "We have some nice desserts too. You might want to save some room for some of it."

"I don't care for sweets, if that's what you call the things coming out of that kitchen." Frank dropped his head and cursed himself for talking too much. When she didn't move, he apologized to her quietly and told her that for now, he didn't want any sweets. "I've had a bad day today, and I didn't mean to take it out on you."

When she left him, he noticed that there was a group of people at the other end of the restaurant that was loud in their talking. The two men at the counter didn't move, nor did they seem pissed about how noisy the place was. He was nearly fed up with it when his house salad was brought to him. He looked up at the waitress and realized that he'd never seen this one.

"I don't suppose you could ask them to keep it down a bit, can you?" She said that she could but wasn't going to. Then she flounced away. Frank was so shocked by what she'd said to him that he sat there with his mouth open until she came back with a refill on his coffee.

The waitress continued to be rude to him for the rest of his meal. Every time she came near his table, she would make a comment about something to do with him. His hair was nasty. His shoes needed polished. And the entire time, he tried his best to keep his mouth shut.

When one of the men from the other table sat down in his booth, he asked him what the hell he was doing. The man was joined by a woman, and they started arguing over the french fries that they'd eaten. Frank started to rise when a young woman sat down with him and pushed him toward the window. He'd had enough.

"What the hell are you doing? I was just leaving after enjoying my meal." The woman sitting next to him told him that he hadn't enjoyed anything but the bread. "How the hell do you know that? Is someone here spying on me for you for some reason?"

"Yes." He felt his balls tighten up when the woman across from him smiled. "I'm Lauren, and this is my husband, Colin. The lady there is Jamie. She can read your mind."

"That's not possible." The woman, Jamie, smiled at him this time, and he was more afraid of her than Lauren. "What is it you hope to accomplish by threatening me like this?"

"We're not threatening you, Frank. Or should we call you Robert? You and I have had some nice conversations over the last few days. That is, until you broke your laptop when you fled the hotel room in your boxers." He asked her what she was talking about, and she laughed. He changed his mind; Lauren was scary, but he didn't trust Jamie more. "Now, we're going to have a nice conversation here and you're going

197

to behave yourself. You will be going to jail. But how you help us now can mean the difference in you being in lock down for the rest of your days, or us killing you outright."

"You can't talk to me that way." He had to think. "I'm a good friend of the President. Once I tell him how you treated me, he'll come down on you so hard that you won't see the light of day."

The next person sat down at the booth, sitting at the end of his table. The chair had been turned around so that the man sitting on it was facing the back of it. It was none other than Jarvis himself.

"We're not friends, Robert. And it's doubtful that we ever will be. I'm interested in some the answers to these questions too, so by all means, Lauren, proceed with this." Jarvis was brought a cup of something, and Frank wondered if it was the same nasty shit he'd been forced to drink.

"No, it's not." He looked at Jamie, feeling every bit as terrified as he'd ever been. "We make that coffee specifically for you since you started coming in here two weeks ago. It's a mixture of coffee and rancid tomato juice. Isn't that just about the worst thing to do to someone? Oh, wait—you killed Iris, didn't you? That would be the worst in my book."

"Who are you people?" Lauren started to tell him their names again, and he told her he wanted to know who they thought they were to be making these accusations against him. "You will be arrested for slander as soon as I'm in charge."

"You really think that we're going to allow you to go through with your little plan of killing the President? And starting a war that will end thousands of lives on both sides? No, that's not going to happen either." Jamie took the offered milkshake that smelled divine. Colin was eating a thick roast beef sandwich, while Jarvis had a large slice of blueberry pie. This was ridiculous. He shouldn't have to sit here and put up with this. "You see that man over there? That is my husband, Hawkins. He's already shot one man today, and if you try and run, he won't just wound you, but will kill you. He wants to kill you, but he's prepared to wait on you."

"What is it you people want? You have no proof of anything, even if it were something that I'd entertain." The papers were slid across the table at him by Colin. He didn't have to look at them to know that they were his notes, and that it was all there in black and white for them to read. "What? A man can't have a little fantasy once in a while? Well, try and prove that to a judge, why don't you."

The recording was of him at Iris's house, the afternoon she'd been fired, and he'd killed her. It was all there, every word, each syllable that he'd spoken. Then several pictures came his way, stills from the night that he'd been in the Oval Office to steal useless paperwork. Then it occurred to him why the name Hawkins was so familiar. He'd been the one that had signed where Jarvis should have, and he and Lauren were the two who' had messed up his plan.

"I'd like to call my lawyer." A cell phone was put next to him. "It would be a private call, so I'll make it from my hotel room."

"What would be the point in that? I can read your mind, so I'll know everything you do and say anyway. Oh, and I'd get that nasty thought out of your head about knocking me to the floor and running. I will hurt you if you try." He asked her what she thought she'd do to him when Colin had the gun. "This."

The fire in her palm had him staring at it in fascination.

And when she made it dance on her palm, turning into shapes like elephants and flowers, he reached out to touch it. It wasn't real anyway, and he wanted to see how they'd done it. When she told him it was hot, too hot for him to handle, Frank blew her off and touched the flame with his hand.

There was no pain at first. Nothing to indicate that he might have bitten off more than he could chew. Pulling his hand back out of the flame, he once again became mesmerized by the flame. This time it was on his hands, and it was burning through his skin.

Screaming about the pain, he pushed Jamie out of his way. His hand was melting—he could see the way the skin dripped off the ends of his fingers and onto the floor. He was looking around for water, anything to cool his hand off, when he was thrown to the floor. It took him almost too long to realize that someone was trying to put him out. But instead of letting them help him, Frank waved his hand around, pieces of him flying about the room and onto other parts of his body. His pants were on fire, the flame of it burning through them and onto his flesh. Everywhere he looked, he was burning up.

"Stop moving, you moron—you're making it worse." Jamie told him over and over to lie still, that help was coming. Frank knew that it was much too late for help now. He looked at the younger man who had joined them and reached out to touch him. But he sidestepped his hand and spoke to the woman.

"End it." She said that she couldn't do that. "If you do not, he'll suffer for the rest of his life, and that is not what you want to happen. Is it?" Jamie shook her head and the boy spoke again. "End this now, or it'll spread to the other buildings once it reaches outside of here."

The woman was suddenly gone, and in her place was a white waving heat that took his breath away. The need to touch it was overwhelming, but he held back. He was hurting too much now to speak, but he could scream in his mind.

When a sliver of her flame reached out, he saw the flames around and on him follow it back to her. The pain then increased so much that he would have begged her to kill him to end this.

The flame came out again, and this time it wrapped around him like a warm blanket. And there wasn't any more pain — the heat was welcoming, and he closed his eyes, or at least he tried to. Everything on him and inside of him was melting, and he looked at the woman who held him in the white flame.

"End me. Please?"

The pain was considerable then, and he cried out. As his face was melting away, he knew that he was going to die. And when he was let out of the flame, he let death take him.

~*~

Hawkins held Jamie as the rest of them went about the business of filling out the paperwork. She hadn't been hurt physically, but mentally she was overwhelmed. Rocking her back and forth as she sat on his lap, Hawkins thought of what he'd witnessed tonight.

Jamie's flame had gathered the other fires around the room, bringing them back to her body, putting out the fires one by one while it seemed to have captured Frank in its deathly grip. When he begged her to end him, Frank was coiled tighter in her snake-like rope of flame and laid on the floor. In the next moment he was gone, just a little ash left behind to show that someone had been there.

201

That was when he realized that not only was Frank gone, his body burnt to ash, but the diner that they'd all witnessed this in was as pristine as it had been before, with a few improvements — new benches, as well as better, sturdier tables.

"I'm all right now." He looked at her face and the tear tracks that were there. "He touched the flame. I told him not to, but he didn't listen. I tried to get it away from him, to put it out, but he had already touched it by then."

"He killed himself. That's what the official report is going to say." She nodded and looked around the room with him. "I'm done with working for Jarvis and Lauren. I think she's going to quit when his term ends as well."

"That's what she told me." He knew that they'd grown closer over the last few days, and only nodded when she said that. "I apparently have a business to run. And four brothers to keep in line. They might just be missing too before this is all done."

"Have you talked to Marshall yet? About all that you can do?" She said that was next on her list of things to do. "I have a friend, a very old and wise vampire. I've asked her to go to Marshall and take the cancer away. I've seen people go through that kind of death, and I'd like to not ever see it happen again."

"Thank you. Will he know?" Hawkins said he'd not because she was that good. "I don't think he'll be able to handle any more surprises once he sees what I can do."

"Yes, I can see that too. The poor man is just adjusting to the fact that he has a daughter, and you're going to show him just how bad assed you really are." They both laughed, and he felt better for it. "How about, Mrs. McCullough, you and I go home and see about breaking in the new bed? We have to make sure that it's bouncy enough for when the kids come in to jump on it."

Hawkins looked back as they made their way to the truck. His brothers were all there, their wives with them, and any children that had joined them. His mom and dad were each holding one of Colin's brood, and they seemed to be the happiest he'd ever seen them. Getting in the truck, Hawkins pulled Jamie to him and kissed her. She asked him what that was for.

"For being who you are and taking no prisoners. My wife, the most loving and meanest woman I know. And love." He kissed her again, starting the engine when he pulled away. "There will never be a dull moment with you around, and I'd have it no other way."

EPILOGUE

Hawkins held his first granddaughter in his arms as he looked around the large room. He and Jamie had other grandchildren, all boys, so this little bundle was the most precious thing he could have ever imagined it would be. When he looked down at her, she was staring at him, as if she were waiting on him to finish what he'd been saying.

"Where was I? Oh yes, telling you about your great uncles. They are both your great uncles and great men. You will come, I'm sure, to love them as much as you get frustrated with them. They can be a little over protective of little girls and women. Not to say that I won't be, but I'm your grandda, and that's my job." She pushed her tiny hand out from under the blanket she'd been wrapped in, and he touched his finger to hers. The grip she had when she took his large finger into her tiny hand reminded him of her grandma. "I'm already madly in love with you, little one."

Looking around the room again, he spied his brother Colin. He was forever the loudest in the room, not with just yelling but with his laughter and his joy. Being a husband, father, and grandda had changed him the most. However, his wife Lauren was still the same bad assed woman that she'd been when she'd first came to this family.

Lauren and Colin had never become the mother and father of their own children. But that's not to say that Colin didn't have a brood of children. At any given time, even now they would take in those that needed them. As did their grandchildren and so on.

"Now there is Parker. He's a great farmer around here. I believe around the world. He had so many new plants coming out every year that there is a grand party in his honor for coming up with ways to make fruits and vegetables more tolerable and with less chemicals." He thought of all the things that she was going to try for the first time. "You'll love your Aunt Reese. I guess she's your great aunt. Anyway, she has been in charge of all the birthday cakes for each of the children since they started coming along. You'll be no different. You'll learn to butter her up too, just to get yourself a handful of cookies."

His mom and dad were talking softly. They hadn't aged a day in all these years and continued to be active around town. Dad still built homes and flipped houses for a profit. Mom was very social, always raising money for this and that, which was needed more and more as the years had come and gone. Hawkins told his granddaughter what had happened here.

"Several years ago, a company came to town and hired all kinds of help. They were going to manufacture blankets and sheets, of all things. We were so excited to have them here that we were supportive of them right from the beginning. But it wasn't until Jon told us—you'll meet him soon enough—that he'd found some dead and dying birds in the forest that we knew there was something terribly wrong." He thought of how many there'd been. How many of the other animals that fed on the birds had died as well. "They were using chemicals that were polluting the air. And with that, the animals around here. It only took us a few days to get them out of here, but years and years to recuperate our losses in animals of the forest."

He didn't know why he'd told her that, but he supposed it was what he was there for. To bring her up to date on her family and news. Smiling at her as she continued to stare at him, he kissed the back of her hand that still held him.

"Great Uncle Larson is still making us all rich. Not that any of us need any money. But we have been very generous with it too. The new school was built only last year. There is a wonderful new football field that most of your cousins have played ball on. He's been a wonderful help to the town and this family. You'll love him too." He looked at Larson's wife, Virginia, and wondered how he was to tell his granddaughter about her aunt. "She writes books. Best sellers, as a matter of fact. But you're never to read her books until.... Well, you come and ask me, and I'll let you know when you are old enough. But don't count on it being anytime soon."

There was another writer in Larson's family. But he had made his way in that world by writing children's books about farm life. The other three kids, all girls, had told their dad that they wanted to work with him, and Larson's business had spread all over the country. He thought that at the rate they were going, they'd be too rich to count it. Hawkins felt that wasn't such a bad thing either, as they had very long lives ahead of them.

Hawkins told her of Dustin and his business. "He has

several hundred men working for him now, all over the state. His housing company has expanded to landscaping, as well as roofing when that is needed. He has finally taken a rest now and spends a lot of his time with his wife, Great Aunt Mackenzie. She's gone back to school several times over the years and has become a renowned surgeon—not that she wasn't already. But she has to keep up with the changes."

Dustin's kids were all different in what they had done in life. There was a teacher at the college level who was very good at it. Another was the point man—err woman—on all the projects that had to do with houses. Her sister helped her, and people were still shocked to see a woman working in her capacity. And yet another of them was working with Parker, raising the awareness of what chemicals could do to a person. He thought that he was most proud of Dustin's youngest two boys. They specialized in building and refitting homes for the veterans that came home needing more than just what the government gave them.

Boyd was the knee doctor. In that he was the one that all the children, young and old, went to when they had a busted knee that needed a bandage. Hawkins thought that he was happier doing that, being there for the kids. Boyd's own children had grown up too—two of them were doctors as well, and one of them had gone into the military just as Hawkins had. "Your Great Aunt Reilly is wonderful. And you'll go to her a great deal, like the others do, when you have a report due at school. You'll never find a better person at research than her."

He looked at his own wife and had to smile. She had never tempered her language, nor had she been any less bossy to him. And he loved her dearly for it.

Hawkins still had bad days. They were a given considering that he'd spent so much of his younger life as a soldier working for the government. But Jamie would snap him out of it. Usually by just being there for him, but sometimes she still knocked him around a bit. She was never one to hold back when knocking some sense into someone would work so much better. And it usually did the trick, he was happy to say.

He thought about his own life. It hadn't been easy, nor had it been all butterflies and rainbows, as Marshall used to say. He missed that man a great deal too. He had been both a savior to Jamie and a good friend to him. But when Jon had approached him about being an immortal, Marshall declined. He just wanted to go out as a winner and a good guy, he'd told him, and Jon left him just the way the man had wanted.

"I work with women in showing them how to defend themselves. It's a good job, and sadly necessary. But I'm very good at it, and the women that leave are healthier and happier. They can not only defend themselves against someone bigger and meaner, but they are good at keeping their children safe as well." He was saddened to think that he had to teach this sort of thing. People shouldn't hurt the ones that they promised to love. "I've recently taken on helping others too. With weight loss as well as training to eat healthier. I don't do that as much as I should, but I've never had any trouble in that department."

He and Jamie had six children of their own, of both genders. All of them had joined the service, feeling that it was their duty to help where they could. But as soon as they were out, not lifers like he'd been, they all married and lived quiet lives and worked as teachers. Hawkins was in awe of them. How they managed to not let stress enter their lives. If he'd had a kick ass mom around like they did growing up, he supposed that he'd be able to handle just about anything. Not that his parents hadn't been there for them all, and God knew his mom had kept him in line, but Jamie had been more for their kids being able to deal with the things that could fuck up their lives. And like his brothers, all of them, he and Jamie had taken in children that needed a guiding hand.

He laughed at the baby when she blew a little bubble from her pretty little lips. She was still looking at him, seeming to understand everything that he was telling her. When Jon came to sit by him, he asked to hold her, and Hawkins reluctantly gave her up.

"Have you been told that she is like her grandmother?" Hawkins told Jon that Jamie had told him. "She'll be someone that will need more than just stories, Uncle Hawkins. She'll need you both to teach her to be careful with what she is."

"I've been thinking on that. Perhaps I could hide her in a mountain cave and leave her there until there are no men around to touch her." Jon looked at him with the most comical face. "I'm joking, Jon. I assume her father is already thinking along those lines anyway."

For someone as smart and powerful as Jon was, he was still learning about the world. It was fun sometimes to just say a random thought to him and watch him try and figure out if it was a joke or not. Jon had never married. No one knew if he'd just not found someone that he could love, or if he just never looked. But that didn't sway him from being the best uncle. He was the one they went to when they needed entertaining. Jon had perfected fireworks that the children and adults loved.

Hawk looked at Jamie when she came to sit on his lap.

"I've talked to Marshall. He said that he was going to bring her to us one or two days a week when she's older. I told him not to wait too long. If someone saw his daughter using her power, it could be dangerous for her." Hawkins kissed Jamie when she glanced at him. "You have that sappy look on your face again. What are you thinking?"

"That I love you more and more every day. That you've taken a broken man and made him into someone that even I can be proud of." She told him that he hadn't been broken, but stupid. Laughing, he thanked her. "But I do love you."

"And I love you, my wonderful husband, who will go into the kitchen and get me a bowl of ice cream."

He set her on the couch next to him and went into the kitchen to fetch her some of the treat that she loved. He found his dad in the kitchen mopping his face with his handkerchief.

"Dad? What's wrong? Are you okay?" He nodded and wiped his face again. "Do you want me to go get Mom?"

"Nah, I'm all right. I just had me a thought, and I was down about it a bit." Hawkins asked him what it was. "That you all grew up to be such wonderful men, and now you're all fathers and grandfathers. It makes an old man like me wonder if you need me much anymore."

Hawkins was shocked by his dad's thoughts and hugged him tightly to his body. The thought of not having his father here with him, for any reason, made his eyes fill up with tears as well. Rich was his dad.

"When I was out on a mission, sometimes for days on end, without doing much more than going to take a piss, I'd think of you and Mom here. Think about what you might have been doing. I rarely knew the date, so I'd always think of

211

a holiday, one that we'd all spend together." His dad looked at him then. "I'd think of Mom running around trying to coordinate, getting us all here on time. Making sure that the table was perfect, and that there were enough places for that just-in-case person that might need a hot meal and a friend to share it with. And I'd think of you, sneaking in the kitchen, tasting whatever food had been left unattended. How you'd be ready with your fork if you could figure out a way to get to whatever it was without Mom knowing what you'd been up to."

"Sometimes when she was too riled up to make any sense, I'd wait until I knew she was coming to dig my fork into something just to set her off. Got her to thinking about something else other than whatever was stressing her out." Dad laughed when he did. "Sometimes—well, most of the time, it would backfire on me a little. But I didn't care as much as she thought I did."

"Do you still carry around that fork?" He reached into his pocket and pulled it out. Hawk had it specially made for him. It would fold over and become too small to be detected in his pocket. "Dad, I need you every day. Not just need you, but look forward to talking to you. Asking you a question that I know you'll have the answer to. You and Mom, you got me through a great many missions. Kept me safe, too, when I thought about how pissed you two might be if I got hurt."

"I'm sure that we didn't know half the times you got that way either, did we?" Hawkins shook his head. "Yeah, well, I don't want to know about them now if you don't mind. Having you home, here, like you used to be is the best thing that's happened to us all. That Jamie of yours, she's just what you needed. Someone to shake you up a bit and not take any of your guff."

"She doesn't, let me tell you." His dad hugged him again and leaned against the counter. "Our granddaughter, have you met her yet? Her name is something that we're all very proud of."

"I heard that. And it is a powerful name that Marshall and his Belinda gave her. Suits her too, since her grandmamma is named for a boy." Her name was Alexandra Jarvis McCullough. "She was named after a great man. I surely do miss him sometimes."

"I do as well." The two of them hugged again and Dad wiped his face. "Are you all right now? I'll go get Mom if you want to dive into that cherry pie there."

Dad turned the pie so that he could see it, and there was a large chunk taken right out of the middle. Mom was going to have a fit, and Dad would enjoy every minute of it.

They made their way back into the living room just as Mom was going in the kitchen. As soon as she yelled for Dad, they both, him and his dad, shared the joke together. It was as it should be.

Before You Go...

HELP AN AUTHOR

write a review

THANK YOU!

Share your voice and help guide other readers to these wonderful books. Even if it's only a line or two your reviews help readers discover the author's books so they can continue creating stories that you'll love. Login to your favorite retailer and leave a review. Thank you.

AWARD WINNING, BESTSELLING AUTHOR

Kathi Barton, winner of the Pinnacle Book Achievement award as well as a best-selling author on Amazon and All Romance books, lives in Nashport, Ohio with her husband Paul. When not creating new worlds and romance, Kathi and her husband enjoy camping and going to auctions. She can also be seen at county fairs with her husband who is an artist and potter.

Her muse, a cross between Jimmy Stewart and Hugh Jackman, brings her stories to life for her readers in a way that has them coming back time and again for more. Her favorite genre is paranormal romance with a great deal of spice. You can visit Kathi online and drop her an email if you'd like. She loves hearing from her fans. aaronskiss@gmail.com.

Follow Kathi on her blog: http://kathisbartonauthor. blogspot.com/

www.ingramcontent.com/pod-product-compliance
Lightning Source LLC
Chambersburg PA
CBHW021957190626
46808CB00017B/2055